CW00435338

ISBN-13: 9798850044718
ISBN-10: 1477123456

9798850044718

Cover design by: Bear & Boo Productions
Library of Congress Control Number: 2018675309
Printed in the United Kingdom

Secret Santa

Holly Green

Blue Pier Books

For Pam, who always brings the sparkle

Secret Santa

Chapter One

Christmas Eve, present day

'Who, the hell, placed these godforsaken balloons around this office?' Charlie impaled a particularly shiny, metallic red one with the heel of her glossy black Manolo.

Despairing that the balloon didn't even make a satisfactory pop when it yielded to her speared shoes, she kicked at another which was dangerously close to accessing her office.

'Come on then, which genius thought it would be a good idea to turn this grown-up working environment into a bloody children's birthday party?' She took in the many balloons in a selection of emerald, gold, white and ruby festooning the office in great swathes. They were accompanied by ribbons in shimmering silver.

The whole effect was nauseatingly festive.

Charlie surveyed the scene. Arms folded in front of her, perched on her sky high black stilettos, she looked every bit the cutthroat editor of *Charm*, the biggest selling monthly magazine for women in the UK. Taking in the rows of white desks all, as she specified, meticulously empty save for the bespoke highly limited edition platinum Macbook, a crystal cut glass filled with water brought in direct from the Himalayas, and a red Chanel lipstick, she congratulated herself on the bare aesthetic.

Her staff looked at her expectantly, but silently.

'Is no-one going to explain this…' she ran out of words

and kicked at an enormous reindeer made out of hundreds of differing coloured taupe, beige and white balloons.

'It's for a children's party,' Charlie heard a voice near her doorway, and turned to see her quivering assistant, Poppy, looking up timidly through her Bambi eyelashes.

'What? Speak up Poppy. Use your grown up voice,' Charlie mocked.

What sort of name was Poppy anyway? She seemed surrounded by staff with the most ridiculous names. All born mid-2000s, it seemed their parents hadn't remembered they'd be saddled with these monikers for the rest of their lives. This year she'd fired a Berry, a Cherry, a Manson, a Dill, two Summers and an Autumn. She was pretty certain she would be adding a Poppy to the list of names of assistant's past, before December was out.

'It's the *Charm* Christmas party for kids, remember?' her assistant said, but Charlie shook her head, not recognising what she was being told, 'for the kids from the children's hospital down the road?' the assistant added in agitation.

'But we never do it here,' Charlie replied, 'what a ridiculous idea. Don't we usually send them a bunch of presents and hire a fat guy in a Santa suit to dole them out?'

She looked at Mel, her only trusted employee. She'd been with her for five years as deputy editor and had never let Charlie down. Mel also never tried to go for Charlie's job, which reassured her that she wasn't so ambitious as to ruin everything.

Mel looked up from her screen where she'd been writing a piece on alternative Valentines, which didn't include red or pink for the February issue.

'We do usually, but fat Santa has got a role in a Christmas show and Poppy here thought it might be nice to bring the kids to our office, to see what a real fashion magazine looks like. She also...' Mel said, using a tone to Charlie to remind her, 'thought her daddy might be able to swing by and give some of the gifts out.'

Charlie groaned inwardly. That bastard.

Still, he did own the company.

'Fine. But they're not coming into my office, and I don't want the sickly little things to touch anything. And I want the whole office deep cleaned as soon as the grubby buggers leave the room. And,' she exhaled, looking at Poppy, 'I want your father to know how thrilled I am that he might consider dropping in.'

She walked to her office, then turned in her doorway, catching the merest hint of one of her staff moving from their frozen positions at their desk.

'As long as he wears a Santa suit.'

Chapter Two

Christmas Eve, present day

'But I don't understand why she's always mean to me,' Poppy spoke softly to Ralph, the most eligible man in the office, 'I try so hard to be nice to her,' she paused to sip her hot chocolate, enjoying the warmth as it trickled down her throat.

'Maybe that's the problem?' Ralph suggested, leaning over with a napkin to wipe the corner of her mouth, 'she doesn't like nice.'

'Thank you, but I can do that myself,' Poppy took the napkin from him and rubbed at her face furiously, 'I'm not a child.' Ralph withdrew his hand, shooting Poppy a wounded look and she softened a little, 'look, it's just that we agreed, didn't we? We can't work together and be together – Charlie is absolutely against office romances, so unless one of us leaves – or is fired,' she added, painfully aware it was more likely the latter for her, 'we need to keep this,' she indicated the two of them, 'purely platonic.'

Ralph sat back, arms crossed over his dark green cable knit jumper, emphasising his strong arms. One of many jewel coloured tops which seemed to constitute his work uniform. She didn't mind though, it gave him a huggable quality. Lean, toned, with long legs and elegant fingers, Ralph didn't really fit in with the *Charm* lot. But Poppy knew he was learning everything he could in the hope he'd one day get the chance to work on *Bold*, the men's title, as editor-in-chief.

Poppy tried to block out the one night they'd been together not long after she'd started at *Charm*. She tried to forget his set of abs that Zac Effron would be jealous of.

Hastily she took a big sip of her hot chocolate in a bid to concentrate on something else. However the miniature candy cane which had been resting decoratively on the side of the glass fell into the drink, causing hot chocolate and whipped cream to slosh over the front of Poppy's pristine white silk blouse.

'Damn,' looking down, Poppy watched as a pool of sticky chocolate goo seeped its way across her top which, only moments before had meant she was in one of the regulation, Charlie sanctioned outfits that were allowed to be worn in the *Charm* office. She began to dab at the shirt with her napkin, managing only to make it worse.

'Here, let me,' Ralph had leant over to help her, a slight hint of mischief in his eyes, and she shook her head violently.

'No, it's ruined. And I have to get to the office, Charlie will be there in...' Poppy looked at the delicate gold watch her father had given her for her 18th birthday, 'oh damn, less than five minutes. I'm going to be so late, Charlie doesn't need an excuse to fire me.'

She stood up quickly, grabbing the well-protected frock she'd been charged with, and pushed past the customers jostling for a hot drink amidst the poinsettias and golden stars that decorated the cafe in abundance, and out into the dark, damp afternoon.

As she tried to stay on top of her horribly high heels, cursing the fact she'd not remembered to pack her trainers that day, Poppy heard her phone ringing from the depths of her bag.

'Please don't let it be Charlie, please don't let it be Charlie,' she began chanting as she dodged the Christmas shoppers laden with bags and stepped off the kerb.

Straight into the path of an oncoming white London cab, decorated, Poppy noted before she blacked out, entirely in red tinsel.

Chapter Three

Christmas Eve, present day

'Boring.'

'No.'

'Why?'

Charlie stood at her desk - to sit down would waste too much time - and flicked speedily through the ideas her team had brought to her for the June/July edition on a screen on the wall.

'I don't like the idea of a bikini spread,' she deleted the page on the screen, 'it's very done, don't you think?' She looked witheringly at the tall woman in front of her, dressed entirely in black, save for a white scarve tied around her black corkscrew hair complemented with a plummy red lip.

It was a look, Charlie decided, which was reminiscent of a 1950s poster.

'Where's the excitement? You promised me bold,' Charlie hovered over the delete all button, and stared scornfully at Mel and the two assistants, Fawn and Leopold, who were both stood clutching their phones and notepads.

Mel moved forwards and removed the mouse from Charlie's hand.

'You asked for a bikini spread – I told you we should do something different, but you insisted last week,' she replied firmly, gaining a deep intake of breath from her assistants and a fierce look of hatred from Charlie.

'Did I?' she answered very quietly, 'well, well, well, aren't we trying to impress our staff,' she looked at the assistants who quickly looked down at their feet, both, she assumed, willing themselves out of the room.

'Well, I say we need something different *Mel* and seeing as you're the Deputy Editor it's about - bloody time - I saw it,' she yelled across the desk. Charlie shook her head, 'I'm very, very disappointed in you. But it's okay, you can make it up to me. I want a full spread with lots of interesting ideas,' she seethed, 'by 9am on the 26th of December.' The two assistants gasped again, and Mel's face fell.

'But that's Boxing Day. Charlie, come on, that means working through Christmas Day,' she stuttered, 'what about my family?'

Uninterested, Charlie flapped her hands in front of Mel's face dismissively. 'Or you could look at it that I'm giving you 41 hours to pull together work which you should have done earlier. Personally I think I'm being lenient. That is…' Charlie pulled on her black, fur trimmed coat, and eyeballed her deputy, 'if you want to keep your job of course.'

Not waiting to hear the reply and knowing full well that she'd see an improvement on the drivel, which she'd seen that afternoon in a day or so's time, Charlie stepped out of the office without looking back. Striding past the mainly empty desks, she grabbed one of the number of skinny girls who did something or other for her magazine, startling her.

'Where is everyone?'

'They're, that is, they're…' the girl stammered and Charlie shook her head.

How could there be so many incompetent fools in one office?

'Yes?'

'They're at the party – for the children,' the girl, who Charlie didn't know the name of, added, 'we moved all the decorations down a bit to the other offices away from, erm, from your office.'

'Went through with it did they? I hope Cole has a nice big Santa costume on, otherwise I'm not going,' Charlie spoke fiercely, and yet again the girl stammered to reply.

'Actually, he's running late. He's called to ask if someone could help him through the doors, he's worried he'll get stuck,' she added, 'I was on my way down to help him.'

'Right you are, well, what's keeping you? Go on then,' Charlie barked. Then, a thought forming in her mind quickly, 'actually, on second thoughts, *I'll* go down to rescue him,' she smiled, which had the effect of making the girl feel like she was about to be caught and killed for dinner.

'Erm, okay, if that's what you want to do,' the girl said uncertainly, 'he's due to arrive in five minutes - he's coming in a cab.'

'And there was me thinking he'd arrive on a sleigh,' Charlie replied irritably, 'what else would he arrive in? We're in bloody London. It's not as if the owner of *Archer Magazines* is going to arrive on a bus is it? Quite frankly I'm surprised he hasn't taken one of the limos.'

She carried on muttering to herself as she made her way into one of the chrome and glass lifts, pausing only to pull her coat closer to herself to ensure she didn't flash anything through the glass floor.

She was convinced it had to have been a man who had designed the lifts. No woman would have said yes to a see-through box where everyone could see whether you were a thong or big pants kind of girl.

Not that she'd ever wear big pants, Charlie shuddered at the thought.

Though she did need to change into the outfit she was due to wear for the Christmas party.

She may not want to be at the bloody thing, but if she had to be she would at least arrive suitably attired.

In fact, her squirrel of an assistant should have fetched it directly from Victoria Beckham that afternoon, she realised.

'Un-bloody-believable,' she took her phone out of her enormous snow-white leather Chanel handbag, noting as she did an odd WhatsApp message from an unknown number -

You shall be visited by three...

And promptly deleted it.

'Bloody spam messages.'

She was just about to phone Poppy, when her phone began ringing.

Charlie was about to hang up the call, but on seeing it was the veteran editor of *Femme* magazine, Fifi Le Swan who had, by all accounts, been marched off to a clinic after a highly publicised torrent of abuse towards a waiter at a recent industry event, accepted it – in the hope of hearing the latest insider gossip.

'Hey sweetie,' Fifi drew out her vowels in a terribly put on trans-Atlantic drawl.

'Hello,' Charlie's own tone was clipped. Professional. Never, in all the years the two had been rivals had she had even a text conversation with Fifi, let alone a phone call.

She didn't want the older woman to have the upper hand though, so felt she needed to control the chat, 'what can I do for you?'

'It's more what I can do for you darling,' Fifi replied, her usually highly made-up face was pale but glowing, her hair pulled into – Charlie almost stumbled in shock, a messy bun – and she appeared to be wearing something resembling an athletic top.

But she was also, and this was the bit Charlie was really worried about, smiling.

'And what's that?'

'What if I were to tell you that I've seen the future Charlie, and I've changed my ways because of it? And that there's hope for you too?'

The lift reached the ground floor and Charlie stepped

neatly out of it, then stopped by a pillar to close down the conversation with this strange version of Fifi as quickly as she could

'Look, Fifi, I'm thrilled you've – I don't know, found yourself? Become clean overnight? Had a fling with a younger man? But I've got a lot to do, and, in case you hadn't noticed it's Christmas Eve and I need to see a man about a raise.' Charlie watched idly as she saw members of staff leaving, their faces flashing on the security screens as each walked through.

'Charlie. It's more. It's better than that. I lost the plot – I was too obsessed with readership, advertising, what Chanel was doing next year…'

'I wouldn't worry, they're not going to tell you – it's only me who has their ear,' Charlie said with satisfaction.

'But that's what I'm trying to say – I don't need any of that now. And neither do you. Charlie, you're younger than me, I won't say how much younger,' the woman smiled, 'but you're young, you've got time to make amends. To be kind, and to learn how to make people want to work for you through choice, not bullying.'

'What? None of that is necessary. My life is fine, thank you. And if that's everything, I must be off,' Charlie shook her head, what was Fifi calling for? Distracted by a flash of something on a screen, she looked in the direction of the security screens. She blinked. For a moment she could have sworn that Fifi's picture was on all the screens, and she was laughing.

When Charlie looked again all the screens were back to normal.

'Charlie, you will be visited by…'

'I don't want to be visited by anyone. Goodnight Fifi.'

And with that, Charlie hung up.

Shaking her head at the odd direction her last five minutes had taken, she smoothed her already incredible sleek bob and took a deep breath in. She had a lot on her plate, which, now she thought about it, included finding Cole.

She pressed call on Poppy's number as she made her way out of the revolving door of *Archer Media Towers*, pushing past other, slower office workers, and headed out into the street to look for Cole. She planned to talk to him about a raise. There was no way she was running the *Charm* ship for any longer, without a substantial increase in her salary.

It had, Charlie thought with a wry smile, as she listened to the dialling tone - become something of her own Christmas tradition, to ask Cole for a raise on Christmas Eve.

He'd always say no, quoting costs, other staff needing raises first and other such nonsense, but usually by around December 29th he would give in as she'd hold up the print run of the next edition of *Charm*, holding it hostage until he agreed. She smiled. It was her only Christmas tradition of course. She didn't go in for any of that other nonsense.

Swinging her bag onto the crook of her arm and narrowly avoiding knocking a Deliveroo kid off his bike, she waited impatiently for Poppy to pick up her phone, but then she noticed what appeared to be a Father Christmas in a white cab coming quickly down the road, on the opposite of the street.

Checking both ways, Charlie quickly crossed the road, dodging cars and motorbikes and a red London bus emblazoned with a *Christmas Spirit* perfume advert, and walked purposely to the kerb, noticing briefly that her idiot assistant was there too.

Rushing to get to the kerb so she could see Cole before his daughter did, ruining any chances for her to have a chat about salaries, Charlie misjudged the speed of the oncoming car.

Her thought before blacking out was that XM4S P45T seemed an odd registration number.

Chapter Four

Christmas Eve, 1994

Poppy looked around the room, taking in the posters on the walls of what seemed to be a collection of similarly posed men in matching outfits.

'*Take That*, but there's five of them, I'm sure we only featured three in last month's magazine.' Poppy tried to work out what was going on by mentally noting all the other details of the room.

As well as what appeared to be an unhealthy amount of posters of this version of *Take That* littering the walls, a lava lamp cast a purple reddish glow across a single bed Poppy definitely didn't recognise. Alongside one wall was a wardrobe with the doors left open, a dressing table covered in make-up bottles and scrunchies, and a chest of drawers stuffed to overflowing with clothes in every colour imaginable. All built from the same pine MDF, but all covered, just as the walls, in posters.

On the wardrobe though, every inch of space was covered in scraps of paper torn from magazines, of various fashions, interspersed with white sparkling fairy lights.

Stepping closer to the wardrobe, Poppy tilted her head on one side to work out what she was looking at.

I know the nineties are back, but at least mix it up a bit, she thought, as she spotted all the photos had women in various versions of combat trousers and crop tops.

She stared in the open wardrobe and was surprised to see a mixture of nineties clothing, alongside some true vintage finds, including what appeared to be some 1950s tea dresses.

Poppy felt a longing for those. She'd always enjoyed the fifties style, wearing the look as much as she could outside of work, and was saddened when Charlie had insisted on the boring *Charm* uniform of white silk blouses, black trousers and black heels. Or, to mix things up, a black dress.

'With black heels of course,' Poppy said, speaking to the dresses but, on hearing a shout from outside of the room, turned to the wardrobe and instinctively looked for somewhere to hide.

'You don't have to do that, she won't see you,' a voice spoke next to Poppy, making her jump three feet into the air and moving to grab a tube from beside the desk to arm herself with.

'Who are you?' she demanded, whilst trying to grab the cardboard roll as she took in the sight of the extremely odd, yet familiar looking man.

'First, you can't touch that – though I'm not sure what you were hoping to achieve with a poster tube,' the man in his fifties spoke, laughter showing behind his bright blue eyes, a faint sound of bells echoing around him.

Poppy reluctantly did as she was told after realising he was right - her hand seemed to be going through the tube.

'Who are you, and why do I recognise you?' she appraised his weathered appearance, the man looked as though he'd walked off an oil rig. He was wearing bright red overalls with a thick oatmeal woollen jumper underneath, and a dark red beanie hat squashed down tight onto his salt and pepper hair.

With a huge smile he revealed pearly white teeth.

'All in good time. But for now hang on, I think you'll like this bit,' he indicated the door to the bedroom which was opening slowly as a girl's voice yelled from the other side of it.

'I am *not* ruining Christmas – you're ruining Christmas *Mother*,' the door was stuck in the doorframe and Poppy could hear the girl cursing as she pulled on it to open, 'I am NOT swearing Mother,' came the voice as the girl released the door and burst into the room, flopping down onto her belly on the bed.

'Hello?' Poppy spoke quietly, hoping not to frighten the girl, who, she judged had to be around 14. And was currently howling into her *Take That* cushion.

'She can't hear you, I told you that,' the odd man said, sitting at the desk thumbing through a copy of a magazine called *Smash Hits*, which Poppy had no memory of seeing as a comparison title to *Charm*.

She walked over to him. 'No, you said she can't see me,' Poppy corrected, and the man raised his eyebrows in amusement.

'So you thought a disembodied voice was going to be a good way of saying hi? Did you? Imagine if she had heard you – she'd have freaked out,' he grinned as he spoke and Poppy felt her irritation with the man rising.

'Who are you? Who is she? Where am I? And what's happened?' Then, Poppy recalled the oncoming taxi, 'oh my goodness, am I….am I dead? Is this heaven?'

The odd man guffawed. 'Funny kind of heaven, complete with crazy teenage girls, terrible posters and the smell of Brussel sprouts,' he laughed and Poppy threw her hands in the air, her frustration spilling over.

'Fine, well, if you're not going to tell me I'll find out myself,' she walked to the door to open it.

'I wouldn't do that.'

'Just watch me…' as soon as Poppy's hand touched the door handle she was flung, violently, back into the room, onto the bed next to the girl.

Who didn't stir.

Poppy sat up, faintly aware her body wasn't making contact with the duvet and scowled at the man in the red overalls who was laughing so much so he was clutching his sides in an attempt to hold in his mirth.

'What the heck is going on?'

Wiping his eyes with an enormous red handkerchief covered in white polka dots, the man looked over at Poppy and shook his head. 'I told you not to do that.'

'Well, I had to do something. Hang on,' Poppy realised the girl, who had shuffled a little so that she was sat up against her dusky pink velour headboard, had stopped crying and was instead opening a sparkly pink and green A5 notebook. She was leafing through the pages at speed.

Poppy realised it was a diary and looked away.

'You can read it, she won't know,' the odd man spoke, 'anyway, it's not like you don't know what it says,' he smiled and mopped his brow with his hanky, before folding it and placing it inside one of his pockets on his overalls. He pointed for Poppy to read the book and, with a furrowed brow, she lent over the girl's shoulder a little to see what she was writing.

But the girl was writing so furiously, head bowed low over the paper, her dark brown hair sweeping the pages, it was impossible to make out whatever she was so concerned about. Instead, Poppy left her and walked over to the odd man.

'Okay, you've had your fun. Now I need answers,' she said, her hands on her hips, frustrated at how out-of-sorts she felt, 'starting with, why would I know what this girl's diary says? I've never seen her, or it before.' At this the odd man looked directly at Poppy, shock written all over his face and his now icy blue eyes seemed full of concern.

'What do you mean? Of course you've seen her before. Look closer,' he urged. Poppy shrugged, confused and looked over to the girl, but it didn't matter which way she moved her own head around, until the girl lifted her own she wouldn't be getting a clear look at her.

'Look Mister, I don't know what's going on here but I can tell you I don't know who she is. I don't know where I am,' Poppy waved her arms around to show the room, 'I've never seen this room before – it's full of nineties nostalgia, but apart from that, I couldn't tell you anything else. Except for the fact I suspect it's extremely likely I was knocked down really hard a minute ago and I'm probably concussed. I'm hoping this is one of those insane out-of-body experiences and in a minute I'll wake up. Probably with a headache. Probably in the rain. But hopefully not here,' she spoke fiercely, then sunk to the floor.

There was a brief moment of silence, when the odd man cleared his throat as though he was going to speak, but stayed quiet. Just then the girl lifted her head, sniffing back the last of her tears and Poppy got a first glimpse at the teenager's face.

'Charlie?' she uttered, recognising the light grey eyes, the slant of the girl's nose and the haughty pursed lips, but the usual peroxide blonde bob was replaced with a beautiful sweep of chestnut brown hair.

'It's you,' Poppy heard the odd man speak at the same time and she turned quickly to look at him, confused.

'No, it's not. That's Charlie I'm sure of it, but somehow younger,' she said and this time the red overalled man had the grace to look confused. He pulled out a red leather-backed notepad, thumbing quickly through the pages until he reached what he was looking for.

'You are Charlotte Anna Kenzie? Age, 42?' the man looked up from his notepad and looked at Poppy, who raised an eyebrow in response to him.

'Erm, no. Do I look like I'm 42?' she replied, 'and be kind. I've just been knocked down by a taxi,' she slammed her hand to her forehead, 'that's where I know you from – you were driving that cab.'

As soon as she said it, she realised how ridiculous she sounded. But then she was in what appeared to be her very scary boss's teenage bedroom. With some sort of Father Christmas fanboy. Nothing she could say would be any more ridiculous. At the silence from the man, she glanced at him to see he was scratching his beard, and looking incredibly confused.

'No, no, no, no. This can't be right, it was meant to be Charlotte,' he muttered to himself, flicking through his notepad to cross reference something, then pulled out what looked like a bulky phone and started moving it up and down Poppy's body.

'Hey, oi, wait, stop that,' Poppy said, pushing the phone away, 'what do you think you're doing? I didn't give permission for that.'

'My, my, my. Well, who would have thought it? I wonder if it was…' the man was typing something into his body scanner/phone, 'but how? This will never do. But I did everything by the book,' he was still muttering, 'are you Poppy Claire Brooks? Nineteen. Assistant to Charlotte?'

'She goes by Charlie. She'd kill us if we called her Charlotte, but yes that's me,' Poppy found she could push the odd man's notebook down to get his attention, 'so, could you kindly tell me, what the heck is going on here?'

The red overall wearing man sat on top of the desk which, as Poppy knew now, belonged to Charlie and studied the two women closely.

'I believe, this is what is known in the industry as "a fudge up",' he air quoted his words and grinned in a way which was meant to suggest an apology, but instead irritated Poppy further.

'A "fudge up", yes, I would say so,' she shook her head, watching Charlie delve into an enormous tub of Quality Street, pull out a green triangle, unwrap it and pop it in her mouth. That was Poppy's favourite too, but she watched on in fascination as Charlie, clearly enjoying the taste, had another in quick succession.

'The Charlie I know wouldn't dare have half a chocolate, let alone two,' she whispered, unable to take her eyes off of the teen, 'hang on,' Poppy stopped watching her boss and turned to look at the man, 'if I'm not meant to be here, and she was,' she pointed at Charlie, 'is this meant to be some sort of *Christmas Carol* style intervention?' she laughed at the possibility, 'and I guess you're the Ghost of Christmas Past?' she laughed again, 'woooooooo', she mimicked a ghost, flailing her arms around until she realised the man was screwing his face up.

Poppy dropped her hands to her sides.

'Wait, *are* you the Ghost of Christmas Past?'

The man raised his hands in a sort of, hang-on-there kind of gesture, which Poppy took to mean she was wrong.

'I'm not the Ghost of Christmas Past,' he answered and Poppy smiled, relieved.

'Of course, I don't know what I was thinking,' she laughed, stopping when he held his hand up.

'But, I am the Ghost of Christmas Past "in training",' he air quoted again and Poppy widened her eyes.

'You are going to have to stop this,' she mimicked the air quotes, 'and start explaining to me what is happening here. You're telling me I've stepped into someone else's *Christmas Carol*? And not just anyone's, CHARLIE'S. As in, my boss's *Christmas Carol*?'

The man stepped forward to shake her hand, bells jingling as he did.

'In a word, yes. And whilst I can go by a job title, I'd rather we go with first names. I'm Nick,' he smiled, 'pleased to meet you.'

'Nick… of course it is,' Poppy rolled her eyes, 'I tell you what, when I wake up from this - clearly heavily induced drug dream caused by a blow to the head - I'm going to have to see a therapist,' she blew out a deep exhalation, 'assuming I do wake up.' Poppy felt a trickle of fear, 'I am going to wake up, aren't I?'

Nick consulted his book, not meeting her gaze.

'Nick?'

'Look, this is my first go at the whole intervention thing. I thought I'd done it all correctly, but you must have got in the way at the exact same time Charlotte did. So, whereas it should be Charlotte asleep somewhere, but aware we're about to help her become a better person, we have you. Who,' he looked at his notepad, 'doesn't need this level of intervention, apart from…' he tailed off as he looked at her, 'well, that doesn't matter right now.'

'Apart from what?' Poppy challenged.

Nick shook his head.

'No, sorry, can't. It's someone else's department, and it's really nothing to do with me,' he looked at Poppy who was sitting despondently on the end of Charlie's bed as she watched the teen pulling out four dresses from her wardrobe, 'but instead we have you here, and Charlotte? Well, we're going to have to assume that if you'd gained some sort of concussion, she's probably doing that on your behalf.'

Poppy turned to look at Nick.

'So, what do we do now?'

Chapter Five

'I'm glad you asked,' Nick said, smiling, 'I think we should do what I was going to do for Charlotte, and hopefully that'll mean that eventually, the system will kick in and either you'll get moved along to the next Ghost, or Charlotte will swap back with you and we'll start again with her,' he nodded, pleased with his idea.

'And what if I say no, I want to go back?' Poppy asked, her head on one side, trying to work out how to get out of the situation.

'Ah, well,' Nick scratched his beard, 'the thing is, a lot of planning has gone into this night, and the other guy – the main one – he's pretty busy with someone else, so I don't want to trouble him. But, like I say, we've been planning this for quite some time, and the wheels are in motion,' he grinned, 'so to speak, and that means, well, you see, once it starts – it erm, can't really be stopped until it's finished, until you…well…*she*… learns to be a better person.'

Poppy sat back.

'But how will I learn on behalf of her? It's not like I can leave a note in her diary to say not to be a nasty person, can I?' she asked, then leant in, 'actually, can I? Would that work?'

Nick shook his head.

'Afraid not. You can't interact with anything, it's basically like a recording. A catch up version of her life, you can't change any of it, because you're not really here,' he shrugged, 'sorry.'

'Sorry. Yep, You could say that, eugh that smell is bad,' Poppy winced as Charlie opened the door, allowing a waft of cabbage air to make its way into the room, 'I see, so I can't touch anything, but I can smell overcooked Brussel sprouts. Lucky me.'

'Mum,' Charlie whispered out of the door and Poppy waited, worried there would be another argument but all of a sudden, in a cloud of Chanel No.5, Charlie's mum wafted in all smiles, clingy red dress and Christmas pudding earrings. As soon as she walked into the room she embraced Charlie in such a fierce hug Poppy could feel the love between the two women.

'Sorry Mum,' Charlie's voice was muffled in her mum's shoulder, 'I didn't mean to ruin everything,' she looked up and Poppy could see the remains of winged eyeliner making its way down her boss' teenage face.

'Don't be silly darling, you didn't ruin anything – that horrible boy did though, he didn't exactly choose a good time, did he?'

'Why doesn't he love me Mum?' Charlie sniffed, 'I've been a great girlfriend, why would he snog Julia?' she wiped her nose on the back of her hand, 'she doesn't even dress well.'

Charlie's mum stroked her daughter's hair and Poppy watched the two of them, wondering where this woman was now who seemed so important to her boss.

'He doesn't deserve you, that's all. You're worth ten of him and he knows it. Personally I think it's great.' At this comment Charlie looked up, anger flashing across her face and her mum hastily continued.

'Great you know he's awful now, before you give him his Christmas present – this way we can bring it back and I think you should splurge on something incredible just for you. We could go to the sales, just you and I. What do you think?' she asked, holding her daughter at arm's length, waiting for an agreement or an argument.

Charlie nodded, 'I think that's a good idea.'

With an air of a woman satisfied she'd resolved another situation, Charlie's mum briskly wiped her daughter's face.

'Now, we've got fourteen people coming for Christmas

lunch and heaven knows where your dad has put the pudding, but I need you downstairs to help set the table,' she started to walk out of the door, 'oh, and Charlotte darling, no-one needs a sad face on Christmas Day, pop a bit of makeup on. There's a good girl. You're not wearing that, are you?' she indicated Charlie's low slung jeans and white strappy vest. Charlie crossed her arms defensively in front of her chest.

'Erm.'

'No,' her mum cut across her quickly, 'no darling, make a bit of an effort. It's Christmas Day after all.' With that, her mum swept out of the room leaving a slightly overpowering scent in the air, and Charlie staring at the mirror.

Poppy and Nick were sat right next to the teen as she slowly wiped her face and began to redraw her winged eyeliner.

'She seems so sad,' Poppy whispered to Nick, still uncomfortable with the idea Charlie couldn't hear her, 'I think she really liked this boy.' They watched as Charlie took out a photo from inside her diary and kissed it, then tore it in half and flung the pieces in her wire bin.

'She did.'

'But why was her mum so dismissive of how she was feeling? She said she loved him, she must be heartbroken,' Poppy looked on as Charlie chose a fifties tea dress not dissimilar to one she owned herself. Red and nipped in at the waist, it accentuated the teen's petite figure and enhanced her curves. She carefully brushed out her hair so it hung in soft waves around her shoulders, and finished the look with some red lip-gloss. She looked beautiful.

'Smile.' Charlie spoke to herself, looking in the mirror, 'what does mum say? The show must go on and all that.'

Poppy watched as the teen sat staring, unsmiling, unseeing at the mirror and, on being unable to bear someone looking as sad as she was, stood behind her and placed a hand on her shoulder, resting just above the red dress.

'Just smile and they won't notice.' Charlie forced herself to grin, but Poppy spotted a tear at the corner of her eye.

'You can do it Charlie, I know you can,' she whispered to the girl, who nodded as though she'd heard, stood up and left the room, the sound of Noddy Holder yelling out *It's Christmas* floating up the stairs from the stereo and into the room as she did so.

'So sad,' Poppy spoke into the now quiet room to Nick who was watching her closely, 'her mum needed to give her more time, not shopping,' as she was talking she walked over to the bin to see the photo Charlie had thrown in. She couldn't pick up the pieces but she could see them clearly on top of the usual teenage debris of cotton wool buds and sweet wrappers.

On one half Charlie sat smiling without a care in the world, a daisy crown in her hair, looking to the left of her at the boy who'd broken her heart. Poppy looked at the photo of the scoundrel, wondering who would have done such a thing that close to Christmas, then gasped.

'It's my dad.'

Chapter Six

Christmas Eve, present day

Charlie was dead.

There was no doubt whatever about that. It was the only reason she couldn't move her body, and why, whenever she tried to open her eyes, a bright white light shone hard through her eyelids, piercing her retinas.

She remembered stepping out into the road, trying to track down that idiot Cole, to see his outfit. Just the thought of him caused Charlie's heart to squeeze, and she heard a corresponding beep. Funny. Then there was the odd cab. The white one. Though there was something important about the cab, Charlie's thoughts began to wander as though spirited away. She felt warm. Happy.

'Her vitals are good.'

The bright light hit Charlie's eyes again. But this time it was invasive, snaking its way under her eyelids and trying to see its way into her brain. She tried to shake it away but it didn't want to go anywhere. In fact, she couldn't be certain she'd moved at all. The beginnings of a panic attack were threatening to swarm Charlie. Her lungs felt like they had fire in them and any breath she wanted to draw was coming up short, not quite giving her enough oxygen to make breathing straightforward. Her brain was starting to fog and the fear was taking her to darkness.

'We have her. Okay, she's steady. Just a drop there. We need to monitor her.'

Where was she? Charlie tried to concentrate on the exercise her therapist had given her when she felt as though she was going into a panic attack. Five. What five things could she see? Well, that was difficult. She could see her eyelids. The light. She could see the cab in her mind. Its tinsel. The red.

Four things she could hear. A Christmas song. Mariah Carey warbling, reminding Charlie of a time when she used to join in and sing at the top of her voice to the song, when it came on the radio in her parents' kitchen. Beep. That sound again. Beep. She could hear that, regular as a heartbeat.

A sound of something inflating like a balloon. As though if she turned over, if she could, she would see someone blowing up balloons. Using a deep raspy breath.

Murmuring. She could hear someone talking, but their words seemed to be underwater. Unclear. A man.

Three things she could smell. Plastic. Bleach. Something metallic. The panic attack was gone, but the fear remained. What had happened to her? Why couldn't she move?

Two things she could feel. Something hard in her nose. And warmth. So warm. Charlie was beginning to lose concentration, sleep was calling.

One thing she could taste…

'Can she hear us?'

That voice again. Clearer now. How long had she dozed for? Was she sleeping? Charlie tried to say something.

'Did she just move?'

'No, they can sometimes jerk a little, it doesn't mean anything. Let's leave her for a moment.'

Don't leave me. Charlie had been on her own for the last 25 years, ever since she'd left home. Keeping everyone at arm's length, working all hours with not a care in the world. There was no one who interfered with her days. She could work all night. And regularly did. She could sit in her apartment eating Ben & Jerrys completely naked. Which she didn't – too many calories. But she could, if she wanted to. She was alone by choice and she protected it fiercely.

Except now. Now she'd like a group of people around her,

holding her. She wanted to feel something, to know someone was there too, so she wouldn't feel the thing she'd been afraid of for years. The thing she worked at so hard to avoid. Being lonely.

'I don't know, she should have someone with her.'

That voice. Yes, Charlie screamed at the voice. For the first time in my adult life I need something from someone. Please stay. I'm scared. I remember you. Stay.

'Are you her partner?'

A pause. Charlie listened, interested. It seemed unlikely. But then she could be trapped in a dream, so anything was possible.

'No.' Spoken firmly, Charlie experienced a disappointment she couldn't pin down. Beep.

'I think she needs a little more.'

A blissful pink cloud pushed into Charlie's brain. It was mushy like a marshmallow and she smiled, swimming towards it. She could hear Mariah singing to her, all she wanted for Christmas was him too. The pink cloud spread into a magical, ethereal blue white light, it was delicious and she wanted to push towards it. The white light was good. Comforting.

Maybe she *was* dead.

Charlie tried to organise her thoughts, the issue was that she was sure that *if* she was dead, IF, and if heaven and hell existed, then this white light meant she was heading to the pearly gates and there surely had to be a problem.

She should be going to hell.

Chapter Seven

Christmas Eve, 1998

'They're going to hate me.'

Poppy looked on as Charlie spoke into a chunky mobile phone that she recognised as a Nokia – Ralph had one in the present day as a way of being anti-smartphone. With the thought of Ralph, Poppy's heart leapt a little. Whenever she got out of this fever dream – if she did – she had to make a go of it with him. He was such a genuine, kind and caring man, and it didn't hurt he was achingly gorgeous too.

'You've got a weird look on your face,' Nick said, hovering next to her, 'you okay?'

Attempting to focus on something other than the feeling of Ralph's tight torso against her own, softer middle, Poppy pulled her attention to Charlie, realising they weren't in her bedroom anymore.

'Wait. Where are we?'

Nick looked around as if he hadn't realised they'd moved either, removed his phone-scanner and clicked a few buttons. Then smiled when it became clear.

'Ah, yes, of course. We're in the carpark of The Good Companions, somewhere on the South Coast,' he nodded, 'and it's Christmas Eve – of course,' he grinned and Poppy rolled her eyes.

'You can tell me the pub, but not where we are?'

Nick looked a little uncomfortable.

'Actually,' he pointed behind her to a huge dark green sign, emblazoned with the name of the pub in gold lettering,

'I've only got a rough location on this, it's got a few bugs to fix,' he explained, indicating his techy gadget.

'What year?

'1998, I know that because that's the year Charlie went to university and we felt it was a significant moment to revisit...' Nick began and Poppy smiled.

'Okay, well that's nice,' Poppy was reminded of her time at Edinburgh University. She'd enjoyed her course in fashion design and had made lifelong friends with three of the girls there.

'...and decided to ditch it after two months as she'd been invited to work on a fashion magazine in London as an apprentice.'

'Ah. And am I right in guessing it's not going to go down well?'

Nick grimaced.

'You could say that,' he nodded in Charlie's direction as she punched in a number into her phone, tucking it into the crook of her neck as she pulled out a small notebook from her worn black leather biker jacket and flicked to a certain page. Poppy raised her eyebrows and Nick nodded, indicating they could walk over towards Charlie, whose teeth were chattering in the cold.

'Why can't I feel the temperature?' Poppy said, realising she was in the same outfit she'd got knocked down in, complete with beige trench coat. But judging by the ice on the floor she should have been feeling much, much colder.

'I've told you. You're not really here – you're in her memory,' now it was Nick's turn to roll his eyes and Poppy smiled, she was about to talk when he raised a hand, 'listen.'

The two of them stood either side of Charlie as they heard the phone click and a voice on the other end saying hello.

'Mum?'

'Hello darling, we were just talking about you – what time do you think you'll be home? We thought we would have seen you by now.'

'Mum,' Charlie cut her off as quickly as she could and lifted her notepad up, which, Poppy realised had something written in it, 'Mum, as you know, I really appreciate the fact you and Dad have helped me so much to go to university.'

'Yes dear, we're very proud of you – first one in the family to go to university, we're so delighted…'

'Mum, let me finish,' Charlie interrupted, gripping her notepad.

'Is everything alright? Can't it wait until you get home?'

Charlie stood straight.

'Mum, I appreciate you helping me go to university. But,' Poppy heard Charlie swallow, 'a business studies degree is not something I've wanted to do.'

'Well, it is.'

'No,' the edge to Charlie's voice was reminiscent of the boss Poppy knew, 'no, it's not. It's what you and Dad wanted me to do, and I've tried, but it's not me Mum.'

'Oh?'

'No. I can't continue with it, instead I…' Charlie faltered as Poppy read on what she was due to say, 'I have been offered a position on *Yes!* magazine as junior fashion assistant, starting in January,' the joy in her voice couldn't be masked.

There was a silence on the other end of the phone.

'Let me get your Father.'

Charlie jigged around on the spot. Whether the agitation was from the cold that her leather jacket wasn't keeping out, or the impending conversation, Poppy couldn't be certain.

'Charlotte?' a mellow voice came on the line, 'what's this nonsense your mother is telling me? Tell me you're not ditching university in favour of some whim.'

'Dad, it's not a whim. It's fashion. I want a career in fashion and this is just the st…'

'That is the most ridiculous thing I've ever heard. You will not go far in fashion. Come home, let's talk about it and we'll talk you out of those silly thoughts, and in January I'll drive you back to university. Then you can do a proper degree and go into business.' He spoke firmly and Poppy looked at Nick, who shook his head, listening and making his own notes. 'Charlotte? Talk,' her father insisted and Poppy watched the anger chase its way across Charlie's face, followed by sadness.

'No Dad, I won't be going back. I'm sorry, but it's my life. My choice. University is your dream, not mine and I won't be going back in January. I'll be starting my paid internship at *Yes!* whether you support me or not,' she said quietly but firmly, and Poppy mentally high-fived her on making the right decision.

'Then don't come back for Christmas,' the words were spoken in such an icy way, even Poppy felt the cold and Charlie looked suitably shocked.

'What?' she gripped her phone, as though holding it tighter would make everything make sense.

'That's why you've called, isn't it? You're probably not even in town.' Charlie looked at the local pub and Poppy knew she was, 'you don't want to come back, you've called so you don't have to have the conversation face-to-face, you'd rather be off gallivanting with stupid airhead models in London. So I've made it easier for you,' came the words and Charlie sunk down, her jeans darkening as she sat on the wet floor.

'But Da…'

'No, if our plans for your future aren't good enough for you, then you've made your choice. I'm very disappointed in you, so is your mother. I hope you feel proud of the decision you've made,' there was a pause as Poppy felt Charlie's life crossroads hover in the words which were about to be said, 'goodbye Charlotte,' the call rung off leaving the dead air behind as her boss continued to clutch the phone to her ear. Slowly her hand moved down and she began softly sobbing into her soft white scarf.

Poppy sat down next to Charlie and wished she could embrace her but then was distracted by an odd sensation of a warmth coursing through her hands and brain, as though she was being filled up with a tingly juice, which ebbed and flowed through her veins. Leaving her to feel as though she'd had a glass of champagne on an empty stomach.

'Why would he do that?' she spoke to Nick who was considering Charlie, her face sunk deep into her hands, and he shook his head.

'Parents are just people. They can make mistakes just as much as children can. It's just we have to hope they come to their senses a little quicker, with as few repercussions as possible,' he explained charitably.

'Hmm,' Poppy was still unconvinced, 'I'm not sure my parents would ever say I couldn't come home for Christmas, whatever I'd done,' she suddenly winced, a pain going through her head, 'are they okay Nick? My parents? Have I died on Christmas Eve?' She was suddenly terrified at what her mum and dad were dealing with when they should be at their big Christmas Eve party. It was a tradition they'd had for years. Her dad would do his bit at the *Charm* children's party, then he'd come to their house, where her mother would have been arguing with caterers all day, and Poppy's whole home would have been transformed into a winter wonderland.

Cocktails would flow, champagne drunk and tales told of the previous year. It was a time for her parents and their friends to catch up at the end of the year, and gradually it had become a reunion for the kids Poppy had grown up with, to move on from eating all the sweets her mum used to buy in, to stealing the spirits, to enjoying a few sensible glasses of champers whilst exclaiming over each other's various engagements, promotions, babies and mortgages. It didn't even matter that her parents were divorced, had been for five years, they were good friends and they seemed to enjoy the Christmas party as much as anyone else did.

Poppy had been looking forward to bringing Ralph. Though, now she thought of it, she wasn't sure she'd invited him. She would remedy that as soon as she was back. She wanted to show him off. Suddenly, Poppy felt a warm weight on her shoulder and she looked to where Nick was standing behind her, looking concerned.

'You're not dead. I promise. I'm just not sure why you're here, or how. But you're not dead – and my team are working on it,' he smiled, hoping to cheer her, 'look.' Poppy watched as Charlie wiped her eyes with her scarf, leaving black makeup trails across the snow white wool.

She stood up, dusting off the frost from her legs and looked every bit as Poppy knew her now. Picking up her phone from where it had slid to the floor previously, she pressed a button and it immediately connected to a number, someone in her speed dial.

'Cole, can I come to yours?'

Chapter Eight

Christmas Eve, present day

Charlie had an odd sense that her legs were cold.

She could smell salty sea air and the feel of her old biker jacket as she walked into the warmth of The Good Companions. Funny, she hadn't thought of that pub for years. Or seen that jacket for a long time.

She wondered what had happened to it.

'She's stabilised.'

'Charlie, hey, it's me.' She smiled. Cole was on the phone telling her it was okay. She could come to his house, his parents would be thrilled to have her there on Christmas Day. No, she didn't need to bring anything.

Odd, she'd forgotten in the years which had passed, how close they'd been once. Even after they'd split up, and she'd been so desperately, embarrassingly sad, at finding out he'd snogged some other girl.

But when they'd met again at a party of a mutual friend they'd begun talking and Charlie had discovered Cole had begun a fledgling magazine, which was attracting attention for its inventiveness.

'Wake up Charlie.'

They'd been such good friends. When did it stop? Why?

Beep.

So tired. The pink marshmallow was entering her brain again, she was losing his voice into the mush. The smell of the sea air was being replaced by bleach, her jacket disintegrating into a soft blanket as she scrabbled to hold onto the memory.

At least the warmth of the pub was there still, but the lights were odd. Bright.

'Charlotte,' the voice faded.

Chapter Nine

Christmas Eve, 1999

'Do you really think planes will fall out of the sky when the clock strikes midnight in a few days' time?' Charlie held her sides, she was laughing so much, 'come on Cole, that's ridiculous.'

'It's not,' he was sat next to her in a booth of the pub near to his flat, 'it's the Millennium Bug, everyone's worried about. Why do you think Microsoft have been adding updates? It could be the end of the world.'

Charlie rolled her eyes. She'd been hearing this panic from across the media and had even, albeit grudgingly, agreed to cover it as an article for *Yes!* magazine. The whole thing was preposterous and she was not one of those people who was going to be on top of a roof on New Year's Eve waiting for aliens to land, or watch the sky crack open or whatever the doomsayers had been forecasting.

She sighed.

Beep.

'Sorry, am I boring you?' Cole's eyes glittered in the candlelight of the pub that was overly furnished with old photographs and even older books. She looked at him.

In the past year they'd been inseparable, and as her boss, she was thankful for the job into an industry she was passionate about. But as her boyfriend, she was beginning to have doubts.

'No, you're not boring me. It's just this talk of the Millennium Bug, it's so stupid,' she replied, not thinking about the words she was using, instead draining her vodka and tonic and half listening to the guitarist playing a cover of *Last Christmas*.

Beep.

'Hey, you know I don't like that – I'm not dumb, I'm not the only one who's worried,' Cole dropped her hand from where he'd been holding it across the table, 'I run a successful business, I'm just preparing for the worst.'

Looking across the table, Charlie gazed at Cole before replying. He was achingly handsome. Every time she caught sight of the stubble on his chiselled jaw line, the swoop of dark blonde hair he would push his hands through when he was worried, or look into his intensely green eyes, she couldn't believe how her last year had turned out.

Not only had he given her a job, getting her away from the horrible university course she didn't want to do, but when she'd arrived in tears at his flat that sad Christmas Eve a year ago, he had run her a hot bath, poured her an ice cold glass of champagne and, when she'd soaked the pain away and was looking for a towel, wrapped her up in the softest of cashmere.

They'd barely been apart since and for a while Charlie had harboured thoughts they were in it for the long haul. Marriage even.

Beep.

She shook her head, that sound was so insistent.

The truth was she wasn't sure what they had time for each other anymore. She had ambitions to move up the ranks of the magazine, whilst he seemed interested in swelling the magazine group and was in talks to buy up other titles. They spent maybe one night a week with each other now, and even then she was keen to get to work the next morning.

His looks were a problem too.

He knew he was attractive, especially when every woman in the office seemed to have a crush on him, and she had to watch as he flirted with them all. He would always reassure her he was just being friendly, but it made her feel uncomfortable.

Charlie wasn't sure what he saw in her and increasingly she was beginning to wonder whether – other than his looks – she was with him for anything other than a morale boost.

'What are you thinking about?' he nudged his leg against hers under the table slightly and grinned, the sort of smile which used to make her stomach flip-flop, but now she found ever so slightly annoying.

'Not much,' she lied.

Beep.

'What's going on Charlotte?' He would always use her full name, never refer to her as Charlie. To begin with she loved it, it was a term of endearment, but gradually she'd begun to see it as just another way he reminded her of her parents. Seemingly wanting to keep her in the Charlotte mould he remembered from school, not letting her grow into the Charlie she knew she wanted to be.

'Nothing.'

'Charlotte, come on. Something's up. It has been for weeks,' Cole leant forward to take her hands in his, they felt trapped within his larger ones and she fought the urge to pull them away, 'I know you, you forget I know every tic, every facial gesture you make. Even when you think you're being blank. I can read you,' he paused, as though building to something, 'and I think there's something you want to say.'

Charlie took a deep breath. Sounds of a busy hospital filling her head.

'I think we should take a break.'

Chapter Ten

Christmas Eve, 2002

'To the youngest ever editor of *Yes!* magazine, Charlie Kenzie, three cheers,' Adam Belfry, the CEO of *Archer Media*, the magazine group which had *Charm* and *Yes!* in its stable, had a glass of champagne raised and was looking at someone over Poppy's shoulder.

She turned to look in the direction he was, hearing three muted cheers, aware of a pain behind her eyes which she tried to blink away. Once her vision had cleared, Poppy spotted Charlie. She was thinner than when Poppy had last seen her, and dressed in a confection of the purest white silk, which wrapped its way around her lovingly, giving her an ethereal air.

Her brunette hair had gone and was replaced with the blonde severe bob Poppy was familiar with, though, she noted, it had been curled in a way to give more than a little flavour of Marilyn Monroe that evening.

'Thank you Adam,' Charlie raised her own glass in his direction, and Poppy wondered briefly if they'd had some sort of relationship, spotting the glance that spread between the two of them.

'Not got many friends, has she?' Nick had sidled up alongside Poppy, pointing out the space between Charlie and the nearest groups of *Yes!* staff, 'humbug?' he proffered a crinkled white sweet bag under Poppy's nose and she shook her head, 'no? More for me then,' he laughed. Then as if he'd forgotten why he was there, quickly checked his phone-scanner.

'What is that?' Poppy asked, 'I've seen you use it but can I see?'

Nick moved out of the way so she couldn't see the screen.

'Hey, come on, that's not fair. You got me into this mess, why aren't we switched back? Could that thing fix it, is it a Sonic Screwdriver like in *Dr Who*?' she asked, going to grab it.

'No,' Nick's voice was sharp, 'you mustn't - it's mine,' he said, shaking his head and furiously jabbing at the keys. 'Ah,' he looked relieved, 'yep, this is the place.'

Poppy looked around and saw a groaning buffet table, piled perilously high with miniature items of food. Tiny burgers nestled with meagre portions of chips and scaled down kebabs. All uneaten.

'What a waste,' Poppy said sadly, 'people are going hungry and they just discard this food.' She reached out to touch a burger, then realised she couldn't, 'I wish I could make sure someone in need got these,' she spoke sorrowfully and Nick looked at her, the light dancing across his blue eyes.

'I think we can do that,' he nodded, and Poppy looked confused.

'But I thought we couldn't do anything with this. It's a memory,' she reminded him and he shook his head.

'It's a memory *of sorts*. Whilst I can't mess anything to do with Charlotte's timeline, we should be able to help here and there if it doesn't affect her. Let me see what I can do,' he crinkled and Poppy smiled back.

'Thank you, I just worry about people, that's all,' she admitted and Nick smiled at her affectionately.

'It's a good trait to have.'

'Not according to my boss.'

For the briefest of moments, Poppy had forgotten where she was and instead had thought to confide in Nick of her woes related to Charlie, her meanness, the tendency to bully Poppy and the other staff.

'That's why we're here,' Nick nodded, looking over

Poppy's shoulder as they watched Charlie and Adam walk over to the buffet table, out of earshot of the other well-dressed guests who, Poppy realised, were keeping their distance from their new editor. Instead they were huddled in small groups, gossiping and drinking champagne together.

'Happy?' Adam spoke brusquely to Charlie, surprising Poppy with his tone. She raised her eyebrows at Nick who indicated she should listen.

'Relatively,' Charlie replied in such quiet tones Poppy had to strain to hear what was being said. She shuffled closer, noting the miniature Christmas puddings and mince pies which also sat uneaten on the table.

Adam rubbed his hands through his hair and over his face, looking strained.

'What does that mean? I've made you editor – no-one your age has ever been editor before in this magazine group,' he began, and reacted as though he'd been burnt with a hot poker when Charlie touched him lightly on the arm.

'I deserve to be editor Adam, you know that, it's just that I've done it quicker than some of the more…' she paused, 'how can I put it?' She thought for a moment, 'lazy members of staff,' she smiled coolly, 'that seems about right. They're all lazy, I'm not therefore I deserved that promotion. Especially over Laura. She glanced in the direction of a striking ginger who was throwing dagger looks at Charlie.

'We both know Laura was in-line for this - she's worked hard, has good ideas, and has the experience,' Adam began, stuttering over his words and Poppy felt uncomfortable intruding on the conversation.

She knew Adam, he was one of her father's greatest friends and between them they had set up *Archer Media* many years ago. Adam was CEO as he'd had the money, and Cole was the chief operating officer as he understood strategy, which had turned out to be a business enterprise that had worked well for both of them.

Charlie was quietly sipping her champagne, calmly looking on as Adam spoke, and when he finished she placed her glass on the table, fixing him with her steely grey eyes.

'Would you rather I told Cole your plans to sell the company? We're still good friends you know.'

Poppy was shocked.

'Sell? Why was Adam trying to sell the company behind dad's back?' she asked Nick, who shook his head.

Whether he didn't know, or couldn't tell her, she wasn't sure, but she was surprised. *Archer Media* had grown from strength to strength for the last two decades, mainly due to Adam's drive and her dad's determination. It seemed odd Adam would stab her father in the back.

'You know that's not true, it's a fabrication that you're ready to plant in his head. Just because he has a soft spot for you. It's a total lie,' Adam's cheeks were reddening.

'Oh really?' Charlie scowled, 'so why were you meeting with Beth from *The Vault Group*? I've still got the photos you know, and they're our main competitors.'

Adam sighed and Poppy tried to make sense of what she'd heard.

'The deal was, I make you editor and you get rid of the photos. It's your turn to make good on it,' he stood stock still, his face grim but determined, and Charlie cocked her head to one side.

'It never was about the group. Was it?' she looked as though she'd just realised something and Adam laughed.

'You know, for a bright girl you can be awfully dumb sometimes. I'm not selling the company,' Adam hissed, 'I'm having an affair. But it's not something you'd understand, is it? Falling in love? You're just a cold hearted scrooge who doesn't care about anyone, as long as she gets her goal.'

He shook his head, 'you know the only reason Cole gave you that internship was because he felt sorry for you? He didn't expect you to say yes, and he definitely didn't think you'd stick around after you split up *again*, but you've stayed much to his, and my surprise. Your blackmail hasn't been the success you think it has, I've only made you editor to prove you're taking on too much.'

He drained his glass of champagne and looked at her coldly.

'I give you six months.'

Chapter Eleven

Christmas Eve, present day

Poppy's head hurt so much it was as though someone was cleaving their way into her brain.

'Poppy darling. My sweet girl,' Poppy's vision cleared as the sight of her mother's concerned face came into view. She was drawn, and paler than Poppy had ever seen her before.

'Hurts,' Poppy croaked, pointing to her head and her mum quickly grabbed a plastic bottle with a straw poking out, placing it between her lips.

'Sip slowly darling,' she smiled, concern creasing her forehead and Poppy did as she was told. At her other side, her dad was stood fear written all over his face. A look that was entirely at odds with the Santa costume he was still wearing.

'Dad?' she whispered and he came to her, placing a feather light kiss on her forehead, as she thought it odd to see her parents in the same room. Whilst the divorce had been acrimonious, they only ever showed up together for their Christmas party. 'Is Charlie okay?'

Both her parents exchanged a look Poppy couldn't interpret.

'What?' she began coughing, her throat so dry she wasn't sure she'd ever have enough water, but her mum was back at her side, offering her a drink which helped to soothe it.

'Can you remember anything?' Poppy's mum stroked her arm, which, she noted had a drip attached to it, as well as a blood pressure cuff. Her mum clicked a button on the side of the bed.

'Don't ask her Kate, the doctor said not to push,' her dad came to her aid and she smiled, then frowned, wincing again. She felt so tired. The pain was going but instead she was feeling floaty and was worried she'd forget where she was.

'The cab…' she tried, 'it was a cab…and *Take That* were there,' she finished, smiling slowly as her mum looked on nonplussed, 'and you were, Dad, but…' her thoughts were becoming tangled as she fought against the sleepiness. Somewhere Bing Crosby was crooning about a *White Christmas*. May the days be merry and bright.

Poppy realised she was fighting a losing battle, she could smell mulled wine and something was pulling her deep, deep, down. Just as she was about to allow the feeling to envelope her, a voice she recognised entered her dreamy, fuzzy state and she opened one very, heavy eyelid.

'Hello Poppy, let's see how we're doing, shall we?'

'You?'

Chapter Twelve

Christmas Eve, 2004

Poppy refocused. There in front of her, on a sofa so white it looked blue, Charlie was sat sipping an enormous glass of what smelled like mulled wine.

'Oh good, you're back,' Nick said, looking relieved to see her as he bashed his phone-scanner into his hand, 'this thing kept blipping, you disappeared for a bit. Actually,' he realised, 'everything pretty much did.'

'Including you?'

'Not sure,' Nick admitted, 'where did you go?'

'I was in hospital, my parents were there. So were you – but you were a doctor,' Poppy realised, frowning. Nick laughed.

'That's a good one. Me a doctor? Who'd have thought?' he laughed again and shook the scanner at Poppy, 'I think it's low on battery, pretty certain that's why we had our little blip.'

'By "blip", do you mean the one where you knocked me down, causing me a severe head trauma, then somehow got me caught up in someone else's past? Which,' she realised, 'I'm back in. I was there, I was back at the hospital – I could see my parents,' she turned on Nick, full of fury, 'but you still brought me back and not her,' she pointed angrily at the Charlie sat on the sofa who was sipping her wine and watching something on TV, 'why haven't you got it right yet?'

Nick settled himself on one of the white leather barstools in Charlie's pristine kitchen and didn't reply.

'I don't think she's ever cooked in here,' Poppy was distracted from her anger by the immaculate worktops, polished so highly she could see the view of London's skyline reflected from the windows. There was an expensive looking coffee machine, all chrome knobs and levers, which was the only thing that looked like it saw any use.

It reminded Poppy of the one they used in her favourite café and she had an immediate pang of longing for her own life, and not whatever this was. 'I bet if you open that fridge there'll be nothing in there,' she noted, looking at the enormous Smeg which was standing proudly in the corner.

'We'll find out, look.' Nick pointed at Charlie who was making her way to the kitchen from the open plan living room. She was wrapped in a luxuriously thick black dressing gown, but this wasn't like the ones Poppy and her parents enjoyed wearing on a cold day made of thick flannel and covered in tartan, this was a heavy velour, so thick it seemed to move Charlie along without her help. She pulled the fridge door open and studied the contents.

Intrigued, Poppy took a look over her shoulder and gasped.

'It's packed.' Inside were all the trimmings for a full Christmas Day lunch, including a turkey, sausages wrapped in bacon and potatoes in a tray ready to go into the almighty oven. There was also cranberry sauce, at least four different cheeses that Poppy could spot, and a heaving vegetable shelf. Numerous bottles of sparkling and white wine nestled comfortably on their respective racks.

It was all Poppy could do to not dip her finger into what looked like a delicious tiramisu. Instead, she watched as Charlie looked over the fridge contents and smiled at what she saw.

'She looks almost happy,' Poppy spoke to Nick who was eating a mince pie, 'where did you get that from? Not here, surely?'

'No, I have a supply with me, these evenings can be quite an ordeal on the blood sugar,' he grinned. 'I need at least one mince pie an hour to keep me ticking over. Want one?' he offered to Poppy and she shook her head, 'are you sure? Might be life changing?' Poppy frowned and shook her head again, 'suit yourself, don't say I didn't offer.'

Poppy watched as Charlie brought a platter of antipasti out of the fridge - small morsels of sundried tomatoes, juicy green olives, artichokes swimming in a garlicky oil, and the thinnest slices of prosciutto ham.

She arranged them carefully on a plate, refilled her glass with another ladle of mulled wine from the pan, keeping warm on the stove and, satisfied she had all she needed, made her way back to the sofa, arranging the neat picnic around her. Just as she picked up the remote control there was a buzz which made Poppy and Nick jump.

'I knew that was coming and it still got me,' Nick said, chuckling as Poppy recovered. Charlie looked at the clock on her wall, a minimalist decorative piece made up of just two hands and some spartanly placed dots, Poppy estimated it was around ten in the evening.

'Wonder who this is? Bit late for a visitor,' she said, smiling, 'unless it's a booty call,' she giggled and Nick pulled a face.

'I hope not. I don't want to be put off my mince pies.'

They watched as Charlie strode over to the buzzer intercom and pressed a button.

'Hello?'

'Charlotte, it's me.'

'Cole?'

'I was wondering if I could come up?'

Charlie looked down at herself and Poppy knew she was trying to work out what she'd need to do to make herself presentable.

'I'm sort of busy,' she tried and for the first time, Poppy wondered why her dad was calling on Charlie on Christmas Eve, 'what year is this?' she asked of Nick who was picking something out of his teeth.

'Erm, 2004. Why?'

'No reason.'

'There must be some reason,' Nick pushed and Poppy exhaled in frustration.

'Well, I want to know why my dad, who would be married to my mum by now, would be calling on his ex-girlfriend on Christmas Eve.' Nick raised his bushy white eyebrows but gave nothing away.

'Cole, I really think you should go home,' Charlie began on the buzzer, only to be interrupted by a knock on the door.

A man's voice shouted from the other side.

'Charlotte, it's me. Let me in.' Sighing, Charlie tied the knot on her dressing gown as tightly as she could, then answered the door.

Cole stumbled into the doorway, his shirt untucked, his tie crooked and his hair, usually immaculately gelled back, had dark loose strands falling erratically around his face.

'He looks so young,' Poppy said, laughing, 'look at him,' she said to Nick who grinned with her as she looked on, viewing her father in a way she'd never seen before.

It was almost 20 years ago and yet, she realised, the only thing that age had affected was his hair. In the present day he was the owner of a slightly receding thatch of salt and pepper locks, not the deep dark hair he was trying to tidy as Charlie poured him a glass of water.

'What's going on Cole?' she said, leaning against the kitchen surface, assessing his demeanour.

'Do you love me Charlotte?' he said, looking deeply at her and Poppy's heart caught in her throat. Had her dad really been cheating on her mum? And with Charlie of all people? Poppy couldn't believe he was such a lowlife.

Crossing her arms defensively in front of her, Charlie considered her response and Poppy waited, holding her breath for the reply.

'We've been over this Cole. I might be a cow at work, but I'm not a cow to other women,' she began.

'You could have fooled me,' Poppy said but stopped when Nick shook his head and held his finger to his lips to shush her.

'You made your choice. You chose Kate. You chose her when you began dating.'

'After you'd suggested we break up,' Cole interjected.

Charlie shook her head and continued.

'You chose her when you proposed…when you married last spring. You've kept choosing her and I refuse to be the one who waits around,' Charlie said, taking a deep breath, 'any longer.'

Cole ran his hands through his hair in an agitated state.

'But what if I chose wrong?' Poppy couldn't believe her dad was ready to leave her mum. Charlie shook her head once again.

'No. You can't do that anymore. I refuse to be a part of whatever you think is going on here,' she indicated the two of them, 'we agreed last week,' she said as she walked closer to him and held his hands, 'we said we were going to move on. Properly. You need to behave decently to Kate. I need to focus on the *Charm* deputy editor job. Neither of us need distractions.'

'She's pregnant,' Cole uttered and Poppy watched Charlie's face as she fought to keep her emotions under some sort of control. Sadness went first, followed swiftly by anger, finished with cool, calm composure.

'Congratulations,' she smiled tightly and turned to the fridge, 'this calls for a toast,' she spoke into the fridge and Poppy noted the tear she swept away as she pulled a bottle out.

'She thought he was coming for her, didn't she?' Poppy whispered to Nick who nodded.

'Charlotte and Cole have been off and on since they were in their teens. He's older, as you know, but not by much and they've been each other's constant. They've both dated other people, but never for long, and they've always returned to each other,' he explained.

'But why haven't they stayed together?' Poppy asked, aware that if they had she wouldn't be around.

Shaking his head, Nick threw his hands up in the air.

'Love is a complicated thing,' he spoke with authority, 'sometimes it doesn't matter how much you love someone, sometimes you'll hurt each other more *because* you love them.'

'Oh.'

'It's a girl, Charlotte. We're having a girl,' Cole was wringing his hands with what Poppy recognised as joy, tinged with worry, 'and I have no idea what I'm doing. I can't be a father – I'm a dreadful person and I don't deserve to hurt another woman in my life.'

He took the glass of wine from Charlie and looked sorrowful as they clinked glasses.

Sighing heavily, Charlie looked at Cole and, on making a decision, rolled her shoulders back and swiftly finished her glass of wine.

'Go home Cole. Go home to your wife, who doesn't deserve to be on her own this Christmas Eve – especially as she's pregnant. Work hard to have a happy life together and every time you think you're about to be an awful human being, love that child fiercely. Protect her, nurture her and educate her. Do the right thing. And I will too,' she added.

Then, before he could finish his drink or say anything else, she placed his coat gently on his shoulders, opened the door and shoved him through it and pushed it firmly shut.

She managed three steps before she sunk to the wooden floor, her chest heaving as she sobbed deeply.

Poppy realised she had Charlie to thank for her dad's constant kindness and forgiveness of her faults.

He was the reason she had never been affected by their divorce. She was showered with love from both of her parents, but he supported her in everything she did. Including recognising she wasn't ready for university and rather than screaming and shouting, instead arranging for her internship at the magazine.

Poppy realised he'd done the same for Charlie. He'd been there for both of them throughout their careers.

The phone rang and Charlie sniffed back her tears.

'Hello?' Poppy couldn't hear the other end of the conversation.

'But Mum, you and Dad promised,' she heard Charlie plead. 'But I've got all the food in and prep...'she tailed off as she nodded sadly, 'no, I understand. If he can't drive, he can't drive. Tell him I hope he gets better soon. Maybe we could try again in the New Year?' she finished with a few goodbyes and hung up.

Poppy looked at Charlie.

A fridge full of food and no-one to feed.

A heart full of love and no-one to give it to.

At that moment Poppy was certain her own heart was breaking.

Chapter Thirteen

Christmas Eve, present day

Charlie hadn't thought about her last traditional Christmas for years, but for some reason, as she lay encased in the woolly tomb that she had come to the conclusion was in fact some sort of hospital bed she was reminded of it.

That was the last time she'd trusted in someone she loved. The following Christmas, when her parents sheepishly asked if she wanted to come to theirs for the big day, after almost ten months of barely a phone call, she declined, saying she had her own plans.

Plans which had included drinking an entire bottle of the most expensive champagne she could get hold of – which was nothing in comparison to the amount she spent on presents to herself.

She'd allowed the shop assistants to wrap her purchases, which included a divine white cashmere sweater, deliciously soft brown leather knee-high boots, and sparkling diamond studs, in all the most ridiculously layered, sumptuous paper they could offer along with enormous ribbons and bows.

She had no tree, instead choosing to place her presents by the fireplace where a fire roared on a screen, and she'd indulged in delicately unwrapping each gift throughout the day. It had become her second tradition of the festive period, she noted. The first to ask Cole for a raise, the second to spend it all on beautiful gifts for herself.

Every Christmas Day for the past twenty years had been spent in that vein and Charlie wouldn't have it any other way. Come Boxing Day whilst the rest of the staff lazed around at home, she'd be back in the office, marking up notes and sending emails, so they'd all have plenty to do on their return – something she felt was particularly important as some of the staff had got it into their heads that the time between Christmas Day and New Year's Day was one where work could slack.

'Not on my watch.'

'Did she say something?'

'Charlie?' that light, the annoying one, hit her retinas once again and she wanted so desperately to close them, but someone seemed to be holding her eyelids up.

'She's reacting to the light – her pupils are dilating,' the voice spoke.

'Thanks doc,' a voice she recognised.

'Nick is fine.'

'Thanks Nick, so how come if all the signs are suggesting she should be awake – she's not?' that voice, it was...who was it...she urged her brain to work properly.

'We don't actually know, I'm sorry – sometimes the body does what it does for a reason, her body must think she needs to be in shut-down for a bit, and until it changes its mind, the only thing we can do is keep her comfortable.'

'Okay, well at least everything looks okay I suppose.' There was a pause and Charlie wondered why she didn't want to wake up. She knew they wanted her awake but something was pulling at her, persuading her to lie still. Something which smelt of cinnamon and pine needles and...

'Humbug?' a rustle of paper.

'I've not had one for years.'

'One won't hurt you.'

Her dad liked humbugs. When she was younger, one of their favourite things to do together had been to leave her mum to her own devices on a Saturday morning, and take a wander into the centre of the small town they lived in.

Charlie recalled holding her dad's hand as they walked, his strides so big she'd always end up running.

He'd swing her up onto his shoulders and they'd arrive at the market full of Saturday traders and shoppers. She'd wrinkle her nose up at the fish stall with its shiny eyed wares that looked at her, and her dad would whip her down onto the floor, then guide her as she danced merrily over to the sweet stall. Every week he'd order the same half a pound of mint humbugs and every week, even though he offered to buy her anything else there, she'd always ask for a gloriously pink gobstopper.

Then they'd sit under one of the trees in the square, Charlie happily sucking on her gobstopper, occasionally removing it from her mouth to see what colour it had changed to. Him munching his way through half a dozen of the minty toffee-like sweets. Once he'd had enough, he'd roll up the paper bag and stuff it into the deep recesses of his coat pocket, for eating throughout the rest of the week. She'd always treasured that time with him. The rest of the week he'd be at work or busy with something her mother had asked him to do. Those couple of hours each week were theirs.

She couldn't remember when they stopped.

Or why.

Although it probably had something to do with her interest in boys when she started secondary school and, a sudden, inescapable need to be fiercely independent.

Meeting Mel at secondary school too, that had been a pivotal moment for her. Discovering someone else who was as obsessed with clothes and *Take That* as she was. They'd spurred each other on with their fashion choices – often spending hours in charity shops looking for items they could revamp, followed by evenings at each other's houses, parading in front of each other on faux catwalks. Charlie felt herself smile.

'Is that a smile?'

'Erm, no, unlikely in the state she's in – probably wind.'

It wasn't Charlie's fault that despite their similar trajectory, Mel wasn't as ambitious as her and had begun to spend weekends with boyfriends – one of which eventually turned into her fiancé and subsequent husband and father to her child. She was lucky Charlie had given her a role at *Charm* let alone promoted her to where she was now, especially as she was insistent on working from home half the week.

The minty toffee scent of the sweets the men in the room were eating reached her nostrils.

Humbug.

Chapter Fourteen

Christmas Eve, five years ago

'Why couldn't you have waited until *after* Christmas to spring this on me, Kate?'

Poppy watched as her dad sat, head in his hands on their chocolate brown couch. She used to love that sofa, it was the perfect size for all three of them to lie on and watch movies together.

'Wait, hang on – we're in my house,' she said, looking at Nick who nodded.

'Yes, and I'm starting to think I know why you're here.'

'Oh really? Nothing to do with knocking down the wrong woman and kidnapping her into a, crazy, festive fever dream?'

Smiling, Nick came over and put an arm around her shoulder. He smelt of pine cones and mint toffee. 'Just listen,' he said, indicating her parents.

'I couldn't wait any longer Cole, I'm really sorry – I am, but you must have realised we were over some time ago?' Poppy watched as her mum sat next to her dad and held his hand. When he looked up he seemed a mixture of a broken man, and as though a weight had been lifted.

'But we're good together.'

Kate nodded.

'We are, we really are. But look, we've never really sparked have we? When we met it was, nice, and you were kind, and a bit like a puppy who needed a home, but you were there and loved me. And our friendship...' she trailed off.

'I don't...'

Poppy watched her mum grip his hand.

'I love you very, very much. You and I created the most beautiful daughter, and I've had so many special, happy moments with you and her. But Cole,' she looked away, holding herself still, training her eyes on the wall where numerous black and white photos of family moments clustered for attention, 'I'm 48, if we stay together any longer I think I might lose myself completely. I need more.'

'More than me. Than us?' as he spoke, he pointed out the photo of the three of them taken that summer whilst on holiday in Barbados, their faces lit with a sunset and for her parents, too many after beach cocktails. It was the happiest Poppy had seen them in a long time, she realised.

'Yes Cole. I need more. To be loved is not the same as to be wanted. You don't want me. Poppy doesn't need me, she's an independent girl and she idolises you.'

He looked up, tears in his eyes.

'But surely you're not going to leave Poppy too? I'll leave this home, this house, but don't take Pops away from her mum, Kate. Please.'

Maggie looked away again and Poppy was stricken – surely her mum had wanted her?

'Actually, I thought we could come to an...arrangement,' she said, looking back at Cole who seemed confused, 'I don't want to leave this house, neither do you. We don't want to leave Poppy – and we like each other as friends,' she hesitated a moment, 'why don't we divorce, but stay in the house together – for now at least, until the time feels right for us to move on,' she looked uncertainly in Cole's direction.

'I don't get it – what's the point? We may as well carry on being married,' he began and his wife shushed him.

'Yes, but this way if we meet anyone, we'll be free to be with them – and the other won't be upset.'

Poppy realised she was holding her breath, waiting for

her dad's reply.

'You've met someone haven't you?'

'Cole, it's not tha...'

'Mum, Dad, I'm home,' Poppy heard herself, knowing she was throwing a bag on the floor as she always did, and kicking her shoes in the general direction of the cloakroom, safe in the knowledge someone would pick up after her. 'Tess was hilarious – she sang so badly off key everyone paid us to leave their houses, best carol singing I've done in years,' she was still chattering as she walked into the living room.

Taking in the scene of her dad with wet eyes and her mum with the all too familiar face that she'd been shouting, fourteen year old Poppy pulled up short.

'What's going on?'

'I remember this,' nineteen yearold Poppy spoke to Nick who nodded, sadly.

'Nothing darling, dad and I were just having a chat. But everything's fine. Would you like a hot chocolate,' her mum had got up and stepped away from the sofa, closer to her. 'I've bought in all the ingredients for our Christmas Eve hot chocolates - marshmallows, mini gingerbread men, whipped cream,' she began steering Poppy towards the kitchen as the fourteen year old looked over her shoulder.

'But what about Dad?' her mum looked in her dad's direction and smiled sadly at her.

'He's coming love, your dad will be right behind – we need someone to reach the special Christmas mugs down, don't we?'

Poppy watched as her younger self looked one last time in Cole's direction and then disappeared into the comfort of the kitchen.

'They didn't tell me until January. Just before I was about to go back to school,' she told Nick, 'and Mum got her way. They lived together for four years, Dad only moved out a year or so ago. But I think it was painful for him, she had a boyfriend almost straight away.'

Poppy went and sat near to her dad, wondering when they'd last been this physically close. 'He worked more. It felt like he was divorced from me more than her,' she lent as near to him as she could, 'I often wondered if it was my fault. Whether they only stayed married because of me and then continued living together because of me. Now I know I was pretty much right.' Poppy wiped her nose on the sleeve of her shirt and Nick tutted.

'You weren't listening properly. They love you so much that neither wanted to leave you – they just wanted to leave each other,' Nick stood behind her and rubbed the back of her neck gently, 'they never thought it was your fault. Sometimes people grow apart, they give all they have to that other person and then they realise one day, they've given themselves too.'

He produced a large handkerchief decorated in holly leaves and offered it to Poppy, who accepted it gratefully and blew her nose. 'We need to hold on to a piece of ourselves Poppy, otherwise we forget who we are.'

Nodding, and feeling a little more at peace than she had in years, Poppy noticed her father staring at his phone.

She knew before she saw the screen whose name would be on it, but the scene vanished before she could see if he called it or not.

Chapter Fifteen

Christmas Eve, last year

'Cole, it's that time of the year,' Charlie said, sauntering into his office, the space decorated with enormous paintings covered in swathes of bright colourful abstract designs.

A large sculpture of a cow head greeted her as she came in. She loathed it, but was aware it had been a gift from an up and coming artist featured on the front of *Charm.* It was, she knew, now worth £1m as the artist had won a Turner prize, and that was about the only reason she hadn't tried to knock the ugly thing over.

For a man who owned a stable of fashion magazines, Cole could have moments of the most grotesque taste.

'Ah, Charlotte. How are you?' he swept his hair from his face a little and gave her one of the smiles which used to make her insides melt.

She batted his niceties away with a manicured hand.

'None of that. You know why I'm here,' she strode over to his desk and placed her hands down on it, barely a metre from him.

'Eggnog?' one of his assistants had appeared out of nowhere and Charlie looked coolly over her shoulder, staring the interloper down.

'No. And he doesn't want one either – revolting drink,' she shook her head as though she'd never heard of anything more disgusting.

'We're fine thanks Fawn,' Cole crinkled a smile at the girl who backed away from the office and scurried away, 'go on then, get it over with – I've got a date to go to,' he sat back with his hands behind his head, the outline of his biceps lightly straining his shirt.

Charlie was surprised he had a date and tried to hide it. Ever since he'd divorced Kate he'd remained surprisingly single, she wondered who had persuaded him to give dating a go.

Ignoring the feelings trying to make themselves known, she looked squarely at him and tried to avoid looking at his arms, or thinking of the times he would pick her up and take her to bed.

'I want a raise. I've increased the circulation once again, the advertisers are extremely happy with the sales, I've brought in more revenue than all of your other editors combined, and quite frankly, I'm owed it.'

'Okay.'

Charlie stood back, surprised.

'Okay?'

Cole folded his arms across his chest.

'Yes, I said okay. You want a raise, I recognise you're doing well – I've said okay. Now, can you leave so I can get ready for my evening?'

He turned his attention to his computer, indicating the conversation had finished.

Charlie stepped back hesitantly turned on her glossy black stilettos and began walking to the door. She'd been ready for their annual interaction. Looking forward to it even. And a date? Who was he going on a date with? Why should it bother her anyway, she had her evening planned.

She turned to tell him how much she…she what? Resented him? Missed him? Hated him?

'Cole?'

He looked up from the desk.

'Yes?'

'Have a Merry Christmas.'

He nodded and smiled at her.

'You too Charlotte.'

Charlie walked through the door, only to be engulfed in a dark so deep she could feel it. So cavernous she felt as though she was falling. So small she felt she couldn't breathe, and so black she was convinced she was dead.

She awoke with a start, sweat dripping down her back and pouring from her face. Her nightclothes were drenched and she felt as though she'd been falling for a very, very long time.

Everywhere around her was dark, but it was a safe darkness. Machines beeped and there was a faint murmur of voices outside. Shivering, she stepped out of bed, feeling wobbly and as though she'd need to break her twenty year habit and eat some chocolate.

Gingerly she pushed the door. The lights out here were bright overhead strips that could only be found in a hospital. A doctor came towards her and she frowned, as much as the Botox in her forehead would allow.

'Do I know you?'

The man, with a curiously long white beard and sparkling blue eyes grinned, before walking past her.

'Hey,' Charlie shouted, coughing as her voice caught in the back of her throat, 'wait, I need some water.' He carried on as though he didn't hear her. Shaking her head, she padded softly down the corridor. She was certain she'd heard voices only a moment before.

As she rounded a corner she came upon a cluster of nurses gathered around a box of chocolates.

'I'll have the toffee one,' a nurse spoke happily, grabbing a sweet out.

'Excuse me,' Charlie's voice was hoarse, but they didn't look up.

'I said excuse me,' Charlie raised her voice. She wasn't used to being ignored. 'I need some water – doesn't anyone look after patients anymore? You all bang on about needing raises,' she started, but realised not only were they not listening –

'They can't hear ya,' a small boy in a curious outfit consisting of a threadbare tweed suit, a faded red waistcoat with a fob watch tucked into a pocket, and a tweed flat cap, was stood next to her chewing on a sweet, 'good ones these – they're my fave,' he winked at her, outraging Charlie.

'Excuse me? How old are you? You shouldn't wink at women, especially not…' she wanted to say women her age, but she was distracted by the boy who was withdrawing the pocket watch, flipping open the gold lid and studying it closely. He was, she realised, glittering.

'Have you come from a fancy dress evening? Do they do that here for the sick kids?'

'Funny. Nah, I'm here for you love. You comin'?'

'For me? Sorry, but who are you?' Charlie was dumbfounded by the arrival of what appeared to be a Victorian street urchin, stood in the very bright surroundings of the hospital. Eating a sweet.

'Oh, where's me manners?' he stopped and took his flat cap off, tucking it under his armpit, and sticking his hand out, 'my name's Bow.'

'Beau?' Charlie was puzzled.

'Yeah, Bow. As in Christmas present?'

Charlie looked at the boy, astonished.

'What did you say?'

Bow continued chewing on his sweet thoughtfully before he replied.

'My name's Bow,' he spoke slowly as though she was stupid or didn't speak English, 'I'm here to help you,' he added, by way of explanation as to why a child appeared to have walked straight out of *Oliver Twist* and straight into the same hospital corridor as her.

Rubbing her head - it really did ache she realised - Charlie felt as though the lights were getting too bright. She could hear bells and assumed they were coming from the music playing in the nurse's room.

'I think maybe I'm not very well,' she tried, before slumping onto the floor. Bow walked over and crouched next to her.

'You're *very* not well Miss. You got knocked over by a cab what was driven by a madman and you've got a nasty bump on your noggins. You was warned though. We sent you that message and your mate, she told ya?' Charlie was completely nonplussed and he looked as though he was going to stroke her head, then thought better of it, 'you'll be alright. As long as you come wiv me.'

He reached out a dirty hand to pull her up and Charlie noticed for the first time that he wasn't totally solid. He had a transparency to him, which was why he'd been sparkling.

'What kind of name is Bow anyway?' she replied, not wanting to go with him though the urge was getting stronger the longer he stood next to her.

'What kind is any name, Miss? Mine's my given name, what they all call me,' he shrugged and, when she didn't take his hand, began unwrapping another sweet before popping it into his mouth.

'Where are you from?'

'I'm from 'ere, aren't I? That's why we've bumped into each uvver, c'mon Miss, you need to come wiv me now,' he spoke with a voice which at once was a child's and a grown man's. There was authority and wit and naivety in it. But she shook her head.

'No. I've not been told what the hell is going on here and I demand to know – people will be worried about me,' she added, and Bow raised an eyebrow.

'Oh will they, Miss? And which people might that be?'

Charlie looked at Bow with the kind of stare that caused

people in her office to be shook to the core. But he didn't look shaken. In fact, he looked amused.

'Watcha tryin' to do? 'av a wee?'

'What? No. Stop it,' she replied miserably, 'I think I want to go to bed. I want to go back to sleep, I want to wake up and for this to be some sort of weird dream.'

'All this Miss?' Bow looked around, his hands raised at the hospital, grinning, 'we haven't even started.'

Chapter Sixteen

Christmas Eve, present day

'Who's ready for the Christmas box?' a woman's voice rang out in the unfamiliar semi-detached house, a call which was answered by a chorus of children's voices yelling their cheers and thumping down the stairs.

'Where are we? What's going on?' Charlie was terrified. She'd been kidnapped and brought to a poor person's house. Not just that, it was a house that clearly was in dire need of a paint job.

Everywhere she looked there was Christmas tat which filled every nook and cranny of the tiny house. Full-size nutcracker soldiers stood to attention either side of the front door and, Charlie realised, the theme – if it could be called that – continued into the rest of the house. Ballerina lights complete with pink netted tutus, dancing mice bunting and what felt like thousands, upon thousands, of twinkling, glittering, irritating multi-coloured fairy lights.

'Enchanting,' breathed Bow next to her, wiping a tear from his eye, 'this 'ere, is what I call, the "stuff of dreams". Wouldn't ya say miss?' he nudged her and Charlie, unsure as to the usual response to a Victorian street urchin time travelling/kidnapping you and bringing you to a pit of vulgarity, nodded.

'Mmm.'

'Let's go in there,' Bow tugged on her elbow but before Charlie could refuse, she was already in the living room, which also appeared to double as a dining room and an office. Everything was clean, she noted, just tired. The walls were covered in scuff marks and crayon stains and the sofa wore all the signs of family life. And the carpet…

'Eugh,' she lifted her foot, noting a hoop that might have been a cereal in a former life was under it, though not - she was surprised to learn - attached to it, 'why isn't this?' she looked at Bow confused.

'You alright Miss?'

'Why hasn't that? Hang on,' Charlie tried to stroke the back of the sofa, 'why can't I touch it? Why can't I feel anything?' she started to panic, 'am I dead? Is *this* what it feels like?'

'Miss,' Bow held both her elbows in his hands and looked up deeply into her eyes, 'you need to breathe. In 'frew the nose, out 'frew the mouth. Alright?' Bizarrely, and against her natural inclinations, Charlie did as she was told, 'feeling betta?' the child asked sincerely, and she nodded.

'A bit.'

'It happens to everyone that we do this wiv, but I fink there was some sorta problem wiv Nick? The first one? I fink maybe he didn't speak to you?' Charlie shook her head, not following any of the questions Bow had thrown out and tried to reason with herself. She had been knocked down. She was ill. Gravely ill.

'Mummy, mummy look,' a dinky girl, roughly aged three or thereabouts, dressed in not one, but two tutus, a dinosaur t-shirt and a pair of gloriously green wellies had bounded into the room, causing Charlie to jump.

'Hello,' she started and Bow touched her arm, shaking his head.

'They can't hear ya. Just watch.' At that, Charlie was surprised to see Mel, her deputy editor and once friend, come into the room followed by two slightly older children. They were all carrying boxes of pizza and the smell, Charlie admitted to herself, was heavenly.

As soon as the children and Mel were seated, the smallest child began what Charlie could only assume was meant to be a dance. She wiggled her bottom, her tongue stuck out to the side with concentration, as she performed a routine best described as a cross between Magic Mike and Irish dancing.

The audience of three whooped and clapped, and Charlie, who had been fairly unimpressed at the performance, couldn't stop herself from smiling at the love that was being shared.

'Are they all hers?' she asked of Bow, who was mimicking some of the raunchier dance moves, he stopped mid-routine and nodded, 'but I only remember her having one.' Charlie said, trying to think back to when an office collection had last gone round, but couldn't recall one for years.

'That's because when you found out she was pregnant, you told her not expect her job to be held open for her if she chose to take maternity leave.' Bow spoke with little emotion but Charlie was surprised at the force of his words. 'So she didn't tell you when she was having more children, and either you didn't notice, or you didn't ask,' he finished, raising his eyebrows.

Charlie scoffed.

'How would I not have noticed her pregnancies? That's preposterous.'

Bow looked sadly at her.

'Like you ignored the other pregnant staff, telling them to suck it up? Telling them to suck it up,' he shook his head as Charlie's mouth gaped open.

'I....I don't remember that,' she finally replied, too late for it to be honest. Bow fixed her with another of his looks that she was beginning to recognise, 'look, if I did,' she began falteringly, 'if I didn't notice pregnancies, well, that's not my fault – they had an HR department, if they needed time off someone would have let me know.' She folded her arms, watching Mel produce a shoebox covered in festive stickers to a chorus of cheers from her children who were finishing off their pizza slices.

'Or they tried to talk to you and you told them if they bothered you again, you wouldn't be responsible for the "destruction of their careers"?' Bow was reading out of a leather bound notebook, but as Charlie leaned over to get a look he snapped it decisively shut.

'What's that? What are you reading?' she tried to grab the book from the boy who was surprisingly strong.

'No. It's not for you to see. The question here is, how come you didn't spot she was up the duff, eh?' he nodded in the direction of Mel, who, at no more than a size ten would have struggled to hide a pregnancy.

'I honestly don't know. I saw the first one. But, that girl there,' she pointed at the dancing youngster, 'she's what, three? Mel wasn't pregnant three years ago. I'm sure of it.' Charlie thought long and hard. 'No, she can't have been because we did that resort wear cover in Antigua and she was in a bikini like the rest of them, soaking up a tan.' She tried to push down the memory of watching her staff laughing and enjoying themselves whilst she'd sat a distance away, covered up to prevent any unseemly tan lines, dimly aware that she might be missing out.

'Which begs the question…' Bow began but Charlie caught on.

'If she didn't give birth to that little girl,' Charlie's voice dropped away as she realised that the middle and youngest looked similar to each other, with their tight blonde curls and blue eyes. Whereas the eldest - a boy - had thick, dark brown hair and brown eyes.

All three were removing fluffy Christmas socks from the festive shoebox, and exclaiming over the terrible designs.

Before Bow could answer Charlie's question, there was a flurry of noise as the door opened and Mel smiled at the sight of her husband James, his overalls covered in paint, his arms weighed down with overflowing Lidl carrier bags.

'Got the last one,' he lent in and kissed Mel on the top of the head, 'though it's that small I think it might be a chicken,' as he spoke he opened the bag for her to look in, causing Mel to laugh.

'What?'

'It *is* a chicken,' she pointed at something in the bag, 'it says chicken on it,' she shook her head at his face dropping.

'I…I got muddled, the letters swam and I just thought they came in smaller sizes,' he grimaced, then smiled at her, 'but, no dyslexic can mistake what this is, here,' he brought out a bottle of prosecco and Mel grinned.

'I thought we said no presents this year,' she said, taking the bottle and smiling, 'but thank you.'

James shook his head. 'I had to get you something love, and anyway, I got paid for that big job today, so we've got something now,' he said, smiling again and Charlie frowned.

'They're not poor. Why are they pretending to be?' she asked of Bow who was watching the youngest dancing again. This time she was wearing her large red Santa socks pulled up to her knees, squealing with laughter when her big brother started copying her.

'Oh, but they are poor miss. They're rentin' and tryin' to buy a house, but saving anyfink is hard, even with both of 'em in work,' Bow explained sombrely, 'people only want their homes decorated when they have money to spare, so James' work has reduced since other people started tightening their belts.'

'I see.'

'*And,*' Bow continued before Charlie could, 'as you've kept Mel on a freelance contract, neither of 'em are a good fit for a mortgage at without a very large deposit,' Bow was checking his book again, ticking off whatever he could see.

Charlie ran her hands through her hair, wincing as her fingers touched a lump on her scalp. So she was here. She wasn't dreaming.

'They're all on freelance contracts, it just makes sense,' she replied, 'I'm not the only person who does this,' she argued, and Bow shook his head.

'According to this,' he looked at his notepad for

reassurance, 'you're the only editor without staffers,' he frowned, 'I don't really know what that means, but apparently everyone has a pool of freelancers, but no magazine runs entirely on them. It says 'ere that you might be savin' money, but you're causing problems in the future,' he finished reading and looked at Mel who was unpacking the Christmas box, 'you mark my words.'

'And the children?' Charlie realised she hadn't had a reply to that question.

Bow looked as Mel doled out chocolate coins from the box, bringing squeals of delight from the children who tore off the gold foil and shoved the chocolates whole into their mouths, beaming.

'They're adopted. After their first, Mel and James were told it wasn't safe for her to have any more, but they decided,' Bow smiled as Mel started blowing raspberries on the middle girls' tummy, making her giggle and kick on the floor, 'they decided they had too much love to give, so they wanted to open their home to other children. This is the second Christmas since they adopted Bella and Rose.'

James came in, this time without the overalls and Charlie and Bow watched as the two sent the children up to bed, encouraging them to clean their teeth otherwise Santa wouldn't come.

'Did you ask her?' he sat, holding Mel's hand on the sofa, both of them listening to be sure that the children were doing as they were told.

'I was going to, but then she insisted we were in on Boxing...' James pulled his hand away from hers and Charlie felt the room lose some of its warmth.

'Mel, no. You promised,' James shook his head, 'not after last year.'

'Last year?' Bow asked of Charlie, who pulled a face.

'It was nothing, I just asked them to come in briefly on Christmas Day to go over a couple of things – they wouldn't have needed to if they'd worked a full day on Christmas Eve, but instead they all chose to go out for drinks,' she recalled.

'Leaving you out.'

'Yes, wait, no, no that wasn't why,' she quickly retracted her words as Bow made an 'mmm' sound as he wrote in his notebook, 'hey, what are you writing? Stop that,' she tried to get hold of his book and he ducked out of her way, appearing alongside Mel and James.

'It's not like that, it just wasn't the time to ask for a raise – there were others in the room and she was so angry at me for the feature,' Mel said.

'Which was rubbish...'Charlie began but stopped when James spoke at the same time.

'Which you'd spent hours on after the kids had gone to bed. Did you tell her that?' James was shaking his head, 'does she have any idea how much work you do behind the scenes? That you're the reason the advertisers stay? That they all ask when you'll be promoted to editor, as they want someone who shows compassion, as well as ambition for the magazine?'

Mel looked directly at Charlie, as though she could see her.

'The magazine wouldn't be the same without her though, she has the most impeccable eye,' she turned to speak to James, 'I know she's terrible. I know she's mean and for some reason she has no interest in other people having fun at Christmas – or at all,' she held her finger up to quieten her husband, 'but under all of that I know there's a good person. She was a wonderful friend growing up. We just grew apart. And don't forget she's the one who got me the magazine job in the first place. If it weren't for her, I'd have given up on writing about fashion,' she smiled sadly.

James leant in and kissed her on the top of her head.

'You're so sweet to see the good in her, when no-one else does. But you're not happy there, and you'd said either you needed more money and more responsibility, or you were going to hand in your notice and go into retail – at least then the hours will be predictable,' he rubbed her back, 'and you'd have exciting things like a pension, overtime, and paid holiday.'

Charlie's body prickled with cold and it felt like the time she'd been invited to the opening of an ice bar, but refused to wear the ugly coat they'd gifted her, so she'd shivered in her Gucci raincoat for an hour instead.

A darkness began to shudder around her vision.

'Mel wants to leave?'

Chapter Seventeen

Christmas Eve, present day

'You can open your eyes now miss,' Charlie felt the now familiar tug on her arm, which meant Bow was nearby.

She was starting to get - if not used to him - then not unused to his presence. Fearfully she opened her eyes, startled for a moment at how dark it was, until she became accustomed to the surroundings and she stuttered in surprise.

'This is my mum and dad's house,' she said, as they stood in front of her childhood home. The windows were dark and it was in stark contrast to the road full of similarly built houses that had something festive about them. Two had given Blackpool Illuminations a run for their money with brightly coloured lights decorating the entire front of each of their houses, right into the gardens where, on one lawn stood a family of penguins – full size – all lit up, and on the other a trio of differing sized reindeers. Charlie grinned at the familiarity.

'That house,' she pointed at the house with the penguins, 'she's the mum of the woman who lives in that one,' she moved her finger in the direction of the reindeer home, 'every year they coordinate their lights,' she faltered a little, 'but I hadn't realised how big they'd gone this year.'

'How would you know? It's been years since you were home,' Bow spoke, looking up from his notebook. Charlie frowned at the memory of the last Christmas she'd been in the road, and carried on taking in the rest of the houses which were decorated in a festive mix of tasteful white lights on bay trees either side of identical porches, or brightly coloured candy canes, inflatable reindeer, and Santa Stop Here signs. All except for her parents', which stood out for not doing anything.

Bow was looking at her, staring at her house.

'Well, ask then. I know you want to.' Charlie crossed her arms across her chest and squared up to the child.

'Ow long's it bin?' he pointed his stubby pencil at her house. She caught herself and corrected her mistake - her *parents'* house.

'Ten years,' she admitted ruefully, 'though I don't know why.'

'Liar,' Bow pointed his pencil at her and immediately they were inside Charlie's house, 'more like twenty years,' his East End accent rounded the vowels, 'and you know why.'

Charlie's thoughts were muddled. Twenty years. Had it really been that long since her parents had called to say they wouldn't make it to her flat one Christmas Eve, and she'd decided never to go back to their house?

That time had passed too quickly. She'd seen them both in that time, but always on neutral ground – afternoon tea at Fortnum and Mason's for her mum's birthday and theatre with them both for her father's but she'd often found the occasions to be stiff, with both parents acting formally with her. And in her case, Charlie felt as though she walked a tightrope between wanting to show how far she'd gone and what she'd achieved but, forever resentful they didn't support her career choice, never offering to pay.

It was her one small win in a battle with her dad, who always looked to her to pick up the cheque, ever since he'd sent her a link to the *Times Rich List* which her name had made its' way on to. She couldn't let go of his turning her away at a time when she needed the reassurance of them both.

'Does anyone live here still?' Bow lit a candle and placed it into a lantern which had appeared with him, it brought a warm glow to the house that was so gloomy and unwelcoming. Charlie looked around the sparse hallway, noting the change in wall colour where her school pictures used to hang.

'What's going on? Where are all the decorations?' she walked into the kitchen, a small pine afflicted affair her mother had always deemed as insufficient for her needs, but which had clearly been as neglected as the rest of the house. Whatever the kitchen had looked like when she was growing up, there still used to be paper chains hanging around the room, looping their way into the dining room next door.

Usually they'd be accompanied by at least half a dozen singing festive monstrosities her mother adored, but which Charlie would rather hammer her own ears out to stop the sounds of Jingle Bells and other nonsense filling the air.

But today there was none of it. No Christmas tat on the windows, no multi-coloured fairy lights that had been brought out every year since Charlie had been born. Nothing.

As she walked back into the hallway, Charlie happened to glance towards the living room, and spotted a glimmer of Christmas hope. She walked into the room, observing as the light from Bow's lantern cast its hue the threadbare grey chenille three-piece suite her parents had bought in the early nineties. It was now worn down so much there was an outline of two bottoms facing the enormous flat screen which dwarfed the room.

'Hold it up there,' Charlie pointed in the direction of the small Christmas tree sat on a dresser. As Bow turned the lamp in its direction she smiled in recognition. A three-foot white tinsel tree stood on the dresser and as Charlie stepped closer, she caught sight of the delicate glass baubles her and her mum had used to buy every year.

Their tradition had been to add a new one to the collection each time. The baubles were a mixture of bright primary colours, alongside golden and silver glittered ones. The angel, as she knew it would be, was the Barbie of hers that her mum had bejewelled one year, giving the doll a golden chiffon skirt and red glittery top, handstitched by the two of them one evening when she'd been ten or so.

Bow had been unusually quiet up to this point, but Charlie realised he was fidgeting.

'C'mon miss, I've only got one more go at this, then you've gotta have some sorta breakthrough, y'know?' he pulled a face which Charlie couldn't help but laugh at.

'What's the rush? You've kidnapped me, I never asked to come along to this trip down memory lane, did I?' she broke off, 'oh, but look.' Bow looked where she was pointing at the base of the tree, 'how did I miss those?' she stopped to look a little closer. There, piled under the tree and sprawling out across the dresser were lots of beautifully wrapped gifts. Oddly, despite her mum's tendency to theme her wrapping each year, these were all different to one another. As she stopped to look a little closer, something odd crossed Charlie's mind.

'Some of these look quite old,' she noted, 'funny, but look,' she went to pick up a present, forgetting she couldn't touch it as her hand passed through the solid cube of white glittery paper, finished with a thick white velvet ribbon, 'this one looks much newer than that one,' she pointed out a long thin box wrapped in ivy green paper, finished with a red satin bow, that appeared to be worn away at every corner. 'And there's so many.'

'Twenty at a guess,' Bow looked meaningfully at Charlie whose perfectly polished eyebrows raised in response.

'Why twenty?' she said then leant against a wall worried she'd fall, 'they're not *all* for me, are they?' she stooped to look at the presents and noticed what she'd not seen before – that every present whose tag was visible, had *Charlie* written on in her mother's cursive script. Those she couldn't see, she guessed would have the same, 'but why are they all for me?'

Bow stared at her.

'I fink you know.'

Charlie wiped the tear which had forced its way out and was travelling quickly down her left cheek, rubbing it away irritably, all too aware there were more coming to meet it.

'One for every Christmas we've not seen each other?'

'Bingo,' Bow spoke, only to be interrupted by a key at the door and the sounds of her parents' voices as they came in.

'We'll need to put the heating on Harold,' her mum spoke as they put their thick coats and hats away into the hall cupboard, 'and I fancy a glass of mulled wine, I need to warm up a bit,' she called, as Charlie saw her dad come into the hall, wincing at the overhead light her mum had just put on.

'Mulled wine sounds lovely darling.'

Charlie grinned as they both kissed under a tiny sprig of mistletoe her dad had produced from somewhere, 'have you checked the messages?' Charlie and Bow followed them both into the kitchen as her mum pulled a saucepan out of a cupboard, and flicked her radio – one she'd had for over thirty years – on to the local station playing Christmas music.

'Course not, I've just got in. Let's check them in a minute, I think we need to celebrate,' her mum replied, 'come on Harold, it's a milestone for us.'

Charlie looked questioningly at Bow who gave nothing away, as she stood beside her mother who was rapidly boiling some red wine, throwing in cinnamon sticks and slices of orange so quickly that the drink she'd been making for as long as Charlie could remember, was splashing up the sides. The smell was incredible though and Charlie grimaced, this was her tradition too - a glass of her mum's mulled wine recipe on Christmas Eve. She hoped she'd get the chance to do it again though, her heart squeezed, maybe with her parents next time.

'Good plan,' Bow spoke quietly in her ear, 'that sounds like progress.'

'Oh, so now you're a mind reader?'

'Amongst uvver fings,' he bobbed a mock bow at her and she rolled her eyes.

'To Harold,' her mum had ladled some wine into a chipped mug which she was now raising in the direction of Charlie's dad, 'for twenty years of bringing a smile to children's faces,' she toasted him, 'as the best Father Christmas in Peacehaven.'

'Ho ho ho,' he laughed, 'if it means a few little ones can get some joy when they wouldn't otherwise, I'm happy to pop a beard on for many more years to come,' he rubbed his belly, which was rounder than Charlie recalled, 'though I don't think we need to go full method on this, I may need to cut back on the mince pies,' he grinned as her mum gave him a kiss. Then he raised his own mug.

'To my darling Maggie. My wonderful, *wonderful* wife, who has given selflessly for the past twenty years. I couldn't be prouder that your gift exchange is so popular, and ensures every child who wouldn't get something for Christmas round here, does. You've helped a lot of kids Mags,' he smiled.

'I had no idea. Looks like me not being in the picture has been better for them,' Charlie said, sadly, 'look at them - helping in the community, setting up a charity, being Father Christmas. They're wonderful, and all because I'm not here,' she shook her head, realising how much she yearned to have a Christmas with her parents again.

'And to Charlie, our darling daughter,' her mother spoke quietly, her voice cracking, 'we recognise we weren't what we should have been twenty years ago. We should have been there, but hopefully, in our quest to be good for other children and to bring them joy, one day we'll have our daughter returned to us.' She wiped a tear as another of Charlie's slipped down her face.

'We'll try again this year love,' her dad kissed her mum on the head and hugged her close, 'let's have these in front of the fireplace and watch *Love Actually* – it's your favourite,' he looked into her eyes, 'we text her earlier, you know how she is. I'm sure she'll send a message to say something. Maybe this year it'll be a yes.' He tried to sound positive and Charlie frowned. She didn't recall a message, maybe she'd been knocked down before it was sent. But even if she had seen it, would she have replied? They'd hurt her feelings for so long she'd given up being understanding.

As her parents walked into the hallway, her dad pointed at the answering machine with its light flashing.

'They must be the only people in the world with one of those,' she shook her head at Bow who shrugged as her dad hit play and all four listened to the message.

'Hello, this is Cynthia I'm a nurse from St Bart's Hospital in London. We've tried calling your mobile but there was no answer,' Charlie watched as both her parents looked to each other confused, 'I'm calling as you're the next of kin of Miss Charlie Kenzie. She's been in an accident and is at our hospital, currently heavily sedated. We think you should come,' the rest of the message was drowned out by Charlie's mother's yell.

'No, no, no, it can't be. She must be okay?' she looked to her husband for her support, but his face was ashen, 'we need to go to her.' Maggie snapped her fingers in front of Harold who sprang to action, 'now. We need to go now.'

Chapter Eighteen

Present day, Christmas Eve

'Ouch', Charlie rubbed her head, her vision clouding as she tried to find her balance. It felt as though she was standing on a rocking boat, and someone with a large stick was repeatedly beating her head.

No, not a stick.

'A pencil?' she grabbed it off Bow, 'why are you hitting me with a pencil? Don't you think my head has had enough beatings already?' she held the pencil in front of him, 'apologise or I'll snap it in half,' she demanded of the boy.

'Sorry miss, I was only tryin' to wake ya, you was takin' ages to wake up and we need to be getting' on,' he replied, by way of an explanation.

'That's a lot less of an apology than I was expecting,' Charlie stood, holding the pencil thoughtfully, 'but I won't break this…yet,' she leaned in aggressively and Bow just laughed.

'You can't anyway, it's a bit more than a pencil. More's than likely it would never break, but still, I enjoyed the passion,' he grinned, 'right, let's get ourselves over to that room – we're in the wrong one, that's why I was tryin' to get you to come 'round quicker. Can't be havin' you in the wrong place now, can we?'

For the first time since coming round, and as she no longer had a pencil thrumming a drumbeat on her head, Charlie realised where she was.

'We're back in the hospital – oh my goodness, are you

taking me back? Am I free?' she held onto Bow's arm. He patted her hand despite his apparent young years, with the authority of an elder statesman. He shook his head slowly.

'I never kidnapped ya miss, did I? Jus' takin' a little trip through your life, offering you a window, if you like, into the world and why you're not usin' your time here as effectively as you could be.'

Charlie was still rubbing her head. She felt cold and miserable and tired. She'd had enough of a small boy taking her out of places and plonking her back into other ones. And she was, she realised, a little more than exhausted of always being angry. It was anger, she was coming to realise, which had kept her away from others. She'd told herself it was ambition and a hatred of other people not wanting success as much as she did, which had driven her forever onwards, never comfortable with staying still.

But she was starting to realise differently.

'For so long now, I think I've been waiting to stop,' she spoke carefully to Bow, feeling as though she could do with a sit down, but realising she couldn't physically sit on anything which was starting to make her bones in her whole body ache. 'I've pushed for more, I've done more. I've achieved so much, but when I'm alone in my room, or when everyone has left and I'm in my office, that's when I hear the thing I hate the most.' She paused, watching as a doctor with her white coat on swept past at speed, accompanied by two people in turquoise scrubs, pulling masks on and hitting emergency buttons. Charlie started walking out of the door, stepping back when a trolley came hurtling towards her with a nurse running alongside, holding up a drip that was attached to his patient.

'She's flat-lining,' he yelled as the double doors at the end of the corridor opened to let the team push through.

Looking at the small figure on the bed, Charlie gasped in recognition.

'That's the girl from my office,' she turned to tell Bow. But he'd disappeared. 'Bow, I know this girl,' she shouted, panic seizing at her heart that he'd left her in some sort of ghostlike state.

'Alright missus, I was just having a peek in this room,' he was poking his head out of a side room, but then dawdled over to her, 'did I miss anyfing?'

Charlie moved towards him, wondering briefly if he was getting younger. He seemed smaller than a few minutes before, 'my colleague, there's a....' she couldn't remember the person's name, 'there's a girl, through there – I just saw her.'

'Poppy,' Bow offered sadly, 'I can't believe you can't take the trouble to get to know her name – you were going to fire her,' he shook his head as he read from his notebook, 'in fact, you were making plans to get rid of her in the New Year, mainly because she was running a party for the children's hospital,' he tutted, 'that's not very festive.'

'Yes, well, I could have fired her Christmas Eve, and I didn't,' Charlie pointed out, though as she said the words she realised how unpleasant they sounded.

'Right,' Bow didn't seem convinced either, 'nothing to do with who her dad is then?'

'Her dad? I don't know who that is,' Charlie lied.

'Liar.'

Just then, Cole ran past Charlie, almost through her - if that were possible - his phone clamped to his ear.

'She's gone into surgery, they don't know what the problem is,' he spoke irritably, but Charlie could see his eyes were hollow with worry, 'one minute she was asleep, the next – maybe five minutes ago, she woke up, said something about Christmas spirit, then fell back and all the machines started beeping,' he spoke loudly, his voice cracking as he tried to hold back tears, 'speak to her? No, you can't, she's gone into surgery – it could be hours, the docs don't know what they're looking for,' he ran his hand through his hair, mussing it up in a way Charlie used to do.

A nurse ran over to him.

'Excuse me sir, you can't use that here. Come on, let's get you a tea and somewhere quiet to sit,' they said, trying to calm Cole down.

'But I want to be in there, with her,' he made to walk into the double doors, after his daughter, and the nurse held onto him.

'I just want to check what your medical credentials are, because if they're anything less than surgeon, I don't think you'd be of any help in there.' He guided Cole away to where, Charlie saw as they followed him, four cosy armchairs sat neatly together in a carefully decorated room that was an ode to warm tones and soft furnishings. Reluctantly, Cole sat down in one of the chairs and sighed, nodding when he was asked if he wanted a cup of tea. The nurse left and Charlie watched as he just stared ahead, looking at nothing.

She was certain he would have stayed like that for hours, if it hadn't been for his phone ringing again.

'Yes?'

'Will his daughter be okay?' Charlie asked of Bow, who was now definitely younger. She didn't know much about children, but she was pretty certain they didn't age backwards. Or glisten, 'you're shimmering,' she added and Bow, to her surprise looked sad.

'Ah miss, that's 'cos I'm goin' to have to go soon. You'll be on for the next part of the journey I'd guess. Anyways, seems about right seein's how's you've not really listened to me, 'av ya?'

Charlie, on for her second surprise of that minute, realised she'd miss him.

'No, you can't leave – I still don't really know what's going on, and, I'm worried about Cole and, erm,' she tried to remember his annoying daughter's name, 'Poppy. I'm worried, see. That's a good thing isn't it? You want me to be less selfish and be nicer to them?'

Bow smiled, his whole body was beginning to shimmer in a way which reminded Charlie of the heatwaves in a desert, and he was rapidly shrinking in front of her.

'Yes, I know. Charlie's in the other room, she's stable but really, what are the chances of having her and my daughter in hospital at the same time? On top of all this, goodness knows how we'll get the magazine out,' Cole's conversation was breaking into Charlie's thoughts, distracting her from the shimmering boy, 'no, I'm more concerned that without Charlie we won't see the February issue out on time.' He nodded and despite her best efforts to try and listen to whoever was on the other end, Charlie couldn't work out what was being suggested.

'Hmm, I s'pose. To be honest, it's made the decision easier though, hasn't it?' he nodded, 'I wasn't looking forward to having the conversation with Charlie about it, but I'd rather she didn't wake up from a coma and find out she's been replaced.' He looked pained, 'no, come on Adam, we said we'd do that in January,' he took a deep breath, 'okay, fine. I'll speak to Mel. But I'm holding you to your word that we handle Charlie my way. We go back and...'

'Handle me?' Why do I need handling?' she asked of Bow, turning to look at him, but he'd vanished, leaving Charlie more alone than she had been for years.

'She's in here,' a short nurse with blonde hair walked into the room, talking to someone behind her, 'oops, sorry, I'm still getting used to the layout – agency staff I'm afraid, lots of people on sick leave,' the blonde explained as she walked back out, 'this is where your daughter is.'

'Oh thank goodness, and is she okay?' a voice Charlie recognised instantly as her mum's faded away and she was torn between staying and eavesdropping on the conversation Cole was about to have with Mel, or seeing if her parents were alright.

'Shall I get us a cup of tea?' her dad was in the corridor and Charlie couldn't help it, she needed to see if her parents were coping. Leaving Cole to his own devices, she went into the corridor, noting as she did an odd tugging sensation like a string was being pulled, which was drawing her into the room where she assumed her mum had gone.

As soon as she walked into the room she was struck by how gloomy it was. Shutters on the window were pulled down and the only light came from the doorway she was standing in. A regular beeping sound distracted her somewhat as she walked closer to the bed, then paused as she took in the scene. There, lying tightly wrapped under white hospital sheets another Charlie lay, a plastic mask attached to her face which was connected to a ventilator that shot regular puffs of air into her lungs. Charlie watched as her chest rose and fell, automatically bringing a hand to herself to see whether the machine was breathing for her or not.

'Oh,' the shock that her breathing was in sync with this comatose Charlie laying on the bed, was enough to make her want to sit down. Up until this point she had been sure she was either hallucinating or dreaming, but now Charlie was fairly certain she was in the in-between space where she was neither dead nor alive.

'Excuse me, hello,' her mum was shouting into the corridor, 'I said excuse me,' she shouted again and the blonde nurse reappeared.

'Everything okay?' she came through, checking Charlie's monitors, a drip which fed into her arm and the ventilator, in one fluid motion.

'Well, not really – something odd just happened. Her monitor just beeped very loudly, and that bit,' Charlie watched as her mum pointed at the screen, 'it jumped very high, and then settled back,' she explained, frowning, 'is that normal?' The nurse peered at the screen, then checked a read-out.

'Goodness, that *was* a spike,' she went to Charlie's still body and lightly pulled back her eyelids, flicking a torch into her eyes.

'Ouch,' Charlie rubbed her eyes and glared at the nurse from behind her, 'every time you do that to her,' she pointed at her comatose body, 'I can feel it here,' she blinked, trying to get rid of the white globules of light which were falling over her vision.

'There,' her mum clapped excitedly, 'there, she did it again – see,' she pointed at the monitor and the nurse looked round quickly to see what was happening.

She shook her head.

'Well I never, I've heard of them coughing, but not this. It's like a shot of adrenaline is going in each time. How odd. I'm going to get someone else to take a look,' the nurse spoke with her head down as she scribbled something in her notes, 'I'll be back in a minute.'

Charlie watched her mum as her gaze returned to the lifeless form of her daughter in bed.

'Hey sweetheart,' her mum drew up a plastic hospital chair and leaned over to pick Charlie's hand up, holding it in both of hers, 'you've gone to an extreme length to get mine and your dad's attention you know,' she kissed her daughter's hand and bowed her head.

It was tough watching her mum crying over her own body and on realising she was trying not to sob Charlie clenched her hand to stop herself.

'Charlie?' her mum's voice stopped her tears abruptly, 'darling, if you can hear me, squeeze my hand again, okay?'

'It's not looking good,' Charlie's attention was taken from her mum as she overheard a doctor walking past their room, 'poor girl is fighting, but it's as if everything is just shutting down,' his conversation petered out as they went further away and she turned back to her mum, who was whispering in her ear. Leaning further in, she heard her mum's ferocious pleas.

'Darling, wake up. This is Mum and I'm telling you to wake up.'

A bustling at the door brought her dad in, bearing two disposable coffee cups.

'I bring teas,' he declared, 'and,' he placed the cups on the bedside table and rustled in the deep pockets of his wax jacket. Charlie couldn't remember a time when he didn't own that coat, 'here.' He produced two slightly bashed mince pies in their foil cups and put them next to the teas, 'they were free,' he smiled at his wife, who scowled back.

'What?' he said, looking shocked at his wife's reaction to pastry goods.

'She's in a coma Harold, but we can at least treat her as if she's here. I could do with a little less of your frugality, and a little more concern for your daughter,' she reprimanded Harold and Charlie watched as her dad went an odd puce colour.

'Sorry love, it's not that I don't care. You know I eat when I'm worried,' he spoke with a mouth full of another mince pie he'd produced from his coat pocket, 'and at the rate I'm getting through them, it's a good thing they're giving them away.' Charlie smiled, he was going to make the Santa belly last all year round at this rate.

'She smiled, look,' her mum gazed at Charlie's still body beneath the bed sheets and talked to her, 'hello love, smile for mum.' Charlie watched on as her own body was unresponsive, her face waxen.

There was a rustling sound.

'This is the patient, doctor,' the blonde nurse from before had arrived in the room, with a harassed looking tall man in a white coat. He immediately walked over to the bed and began checking her responses. Charlie was prepared this time and didn't react when the light hit her eyes.

'Nothing.'

She watched as he placed a thermometer in her ear, noting the temperature gauge rising.

'Normal.' Charlie's mum looked on, reluctantly relinquishing her daughter's hand when the doctor indicated he wanted to check her pulse.

'Nothing of note.'

'Nothing of note? Nothing of note? What does that mean? She's my daughter – everything's of note.' Charlie's mum was tipping into the edge of hysteria and her dad moved round to her, placing his hands on her shoulders to offer support.

The nurse looked to the doctor who was still reading the heart monitor and checking other signs, but showing no enthusiasm for talking to either parent and sighed.

'He didn't mean Charlie wasn't of note. She is. We're just a bit confused. You say she squeezed your hand?'

'Yes, and you saw the heartbeat jump – she even smiled a minute ago,' Maggie added, hiccupping back a sob.

'They do that. Coma patients,' the doctor looked up from the foot of the bed, 'that's all it is. If that's everything I have to go, Christmas Eve is a busy one for us.' And with that he walked out of the room with not even a backwards glance.

'Oh Charlie,' her mum flung herself on Charlie's body and kissed her face, 'darling I'm so sorry. I don't know why we've been so bad at talking to each other this past twenty years. I'm sorry we didn't support you all those years ago. I am. But dad and I are really very sorry – and if you wake up, I promise we'll spend the rest of our lives making it up to you.'

Charlie thought on it a moment. It hadn't just been her parents' fault, had it? Sure, she'd been upset when her dad had told her not to come home, but they'd tried other years to engage with her and she'd pushed them away. A lot of the blame lay with her too. That and the classic Kenzie tradition of pushing things under the carpet, when they should really discuss them. If they'd talked it through they'd have had no stiff, twice yearly lunches and instead had a proper relationship.

'My, can it be true? Cole, is that you?' her dad's voice had an edge to it and Charlie, distracted, looked at the reaction it was having on her boss and former boyfriend.

'Mr Kenzie, good to see you,' Cole extended a hand to shake it, with a very small smile, 'I'm so glad you've come. She's been on her own,' he spoke hastily as he could see them looking upset, 'though I've been in here as much as possible,' he explained, sinking into the other plastic chair in the room, 'whilst my ex-wife kept Poppy company.'

'Poppy?'

Cole shook his head as though trying to remain awake.

'Sorry Mrs Kenzie, Poppy is my daughter,' he smiled, then his face fell, 'she was in the same accident as Charlie, but her injuries seem to be worse. She's in surgery now. We don't know if she'll make it.'

Maggie gasped and clutched her tea closer.

'Oh Cole, that's awful news. I'm so very sorry to hear that,' she paused and looked at her own daughter, alive, if not well, 'do we know why they were there together? Were they friends?'

Looking uncomfortable Cole cast a brief glance at Charlie's body.

'Erm, not really. Poppy worked for Charlie and they were both in the street when the cab driver,' he stopped, stumbling over his words, 'I'm so sorry, it was just such an awful moment. I was in the back of the cab you see. It was so odd. We were making our way down the road, and I'd said to him to pull in so I could cross over to the magazine's building – I was dressed as Father Christmas you see, for the children,' he smiled and Harold perked up.

'Oh, I do that too,' he looked as though he was about to compare Santa tips, when Maggie interrupted.

'Please carry on – I'm sure you can discuss that another time.'

Cole looked a little bemused by the exchange.

'Anyway, where was I?' he rubbed his face with his hands, 'ah yes, I was in the car, and just as I thought we were slowing for the kerb – where I could see Poppy, the driver sped up as though he was trying to knock them both down. Then there was this flash of white or,' he broke off, 'this is going to sound ridiculous. It was like I was in a snow globe – white whirled around and then I sort of, woke up and I was on the kerb. The two women were lying in the road, out cold, and no-one had seen the cab.' He shook his head, 'I stayed with them until the ambulances arrived, then I accompanied Poppy to the hospital. They've checked me over and can't see any signs of concussion, but I must have, because…none of it makes sense.'

Whilst Cole had been talking, Charlie had walked towards him and stood within touching distance.

'I'm so sorry you've had to go through all of this,' she whispered into his ear, wishing he could hear her, and then, because she didn't know if she'd ever get a chance to do it again, 'I'm sorry for being so awful to you all these years. You didn't deserve all of it,' she smiled, 'I hope I can make it up to you.'

Her dad was stood looking out of the window at the London skyline, having opened the shutters. It brought more cheer into the room than the muted light had, but his hands were crossed behind his back and she could tell he was preparing to say something he wasn't comfortable with.

'Look, Cole,' he coughed a little, 'I'm really very sorry about what you've gone through this evening, but we're here now. Her family.'

Cole, if he'd been surprised at the chilliness in her father's voice recovered quickly, standing up and smoothing his trousers.

'Of course. I'm glad you're here for her. She needs you,' he said, smiling at her mum, then, after pausing as though wrestling with whether to say anything else, stood by Charlie's lifeless form, and held her hand in his.

'Bye Charlie, I'm just going to be down the hall – but you're not on your own, okay? Your mum and dad are here,' he lent in and by fortune, Charlie did the same thing as he whispered into her body's ear, 'whatever they say, I have always loved you.'

She stood back in shock.

'Her heart just leapt up again,' the nurse, who'd been listening to the majority of the exchange was looking at the monitor, 'whatever you guys are saying or doing, I'd advise continuing it, she's clearly responding.'

Shaking his head, Cole moved towards the door, turning

the handle and allowing the noise from a busy hospital to enter the quiet room.

'Sorry I need to go I need to find out how Poppy is,' he explained, moving quickly to the door as her father watched them all with interes,t and her mother took up the place next to her bed again.

'Charlie darling, the nurse said we should keep talking to you, so I'm going to. Okay?' Charlie watched as her mum turned to her dad, still standing at the window, 'Harold, you need to talk to her too.'

'Hmm? I will...just watching...' he replied, 'it's started snowing Mags,' he turned to look at her, 'funny really. I can't remember the last time it snowed at Christmas – let's hope we're not stuck at the hospital eh?'

Not looking at him, Maggie lightly caressed Charlie's forehead and spoke to her daughter lying in bed.

'Do you remember the time we went to the duck pond when it was snowing? You were worried about the baby ducks we'd seen in summer, so we had to go and feed them all,' she smiled, 'but when we got there it was all iced over, so you and I had a little competition to see who could skim a twig furthest on the ice. Winner got the biggest hot chocolate when we got home,' she smiled, 'of course you won. It's in your nature darling.' Maggie squeezed Charlie's hand. Standing watching her mum reminisce, Charlie was surprised how emotional she felt and instinctively did their secret hand sign.

'Oh,' her mum gasped, 'she's sending me kisses Harold – look,' Maggie opened her palm up so Harold could see Charlie's hand lightly stroking it. 'It was our sign when she was growing up – if she needed security it was our secret sign she was sending me kisses – it came in handy when she was too grown-up to kiss me in front of her friends too. A quick tickle on my hand, it meant she was kissing me – oh Harold, she can hear me. She can.'

Charlie watched her dad walk over to kiss her on the forehead, and closed her eyes for a moment. She was certain she would wake up back in her body now.

Charlie.

Charlie's eyes snapped open, but she was still hovering away from her body. She looked around for the voice that was calling her.

Charlie, you need to come with me now.

She looked around the room. Her parents were talking to the nurse, trying to work out how she was seemingly responding whilst not showing anything on her charts, but no-one was talking to her.

'Hello?' she wandered into the corridor, looking for the owner of the voice. She couldn't tell if it was male or female.

Charlie

The voice pulled her further down the corridor, towards the doors to the surgery where she'd last seen Poppy go in, *down here.*

She pushed through the door, then wished she hadn't.

A team of surgeons were working on Poppy, but at the foot of her bed was what had caused Charlie to stop in fear.

As hooded and tall and skeletal as she'd ever thought to imagine they would look like.

Death.

Chapter Nineteen

Christmas Eve, the future

'I heard it was stress that got her,' a woman in a very chic black dress, high heels and a tiny hat with a small veil that covered her face, was talking behind her black gloved hand to another woman, who was very similarly, elegantly, dressed.

'More likely being so tightly strung,' the other replied, not quite so quietly, and the two tittered.

'Actually, it was a heart attack.'

'I didn't think she *had* a heart.'

Charlie stood behind them.

'Hello?' she spoke quietly, hopeful in finding out where she was, though she was a little wary that these coiffured beauties would see her in her hospital gown. It turned out she didn't need to worry as none of them turned around. Charlie looked to see if she could work out where she was. It seemed to be a small, clerical room with rows of neatly lined chairs that amounted to no more than twenty seats. The walls held artwork of no consequence, overly bright flowers and cheering seascapes.

'Not much of a turnout, is there?' a third woman, who stood a little taller than the other two spoke as she joined them, 'I did warn her though, if she worked too hard her heart would fail.' Charlie recognised the voice. It was Fifi Le Swan, her arch nemesis. She moved closer and managed to stand in front of all three, then gasped in recognition - the three editors of the magazines who were rivals.

Though, she wondered, for the life of her she wasn't

sure why they'd become enemies when they were the only ones who understood each other. They'd have been better off supporting each other and advising on business issues than trying to take each other down.

The three women sat down on the hard chairs and, almost as one, withdrew their phones from their handbags and began clicking and scrolling, each keeping their screens averted from the others.

Some music started and the women replaced their phones in their handbags, affixing their gaze on something in front of them.

Charlie moved nearer to the front in a bid to try and see what they were looking at.

Then she wished she hadn't.

At the front of the room a wreath of white roses sat beside a coffin, accompanied by a solitary photo of Charlie in a cheap black plastic frame.

'No.' Charlie walked over to the coffin and wreath, 'that's an awful photograph to use.' She looked around for someone to complain to, then remembered the situation she was in.

'Did you hear where her money is going?'

'No?'

'She didn't make a will so...' the three carried on whispering, then laughing mercilessly.

'The children's hospital down the road? Oh that is excellent,' the first one howled, 'she would be rolling in her grave if she knew.'

Charlie did know. And instead of being disappointed at her money going to the children's hospital, she felt relief. Hopeful it would make a change to someone's life – it hadn't done much for hers.

Yesssss.

She looked around for the voice and gulped.

'You know, you could try to be less creepy,' she said, swallowing hard, whilst trying to avoid looking too closely at what the face looked like under the dark hood, 'I refuse to be dead. This is not my life.'

Your life…

'Yes, my life. I will not have it end this way. I refuse. I want more than three mourners at my funeral – unless I die when I'm 100 or something and there's no-one left who remembers me. But right now? I'd expect a whole room of people sad to see me go. At least my parents should be here. And Cole,' she added, sadly.

Something was said and the three women got up to leave, none looking back even once. Charlie shook her head, this wasn't how it was all meant to be.

'I'm a good person really. I'm a kind person,' she pleaded, 'or, I can be a good person. I can be kind. I know I can.'

Death pointed their finger at Charlie and a grey fog surrounded her.

Chapter Twenty

Christmas Eve, the future

'Oh. My office, finally something that makes sense.'

Charlie realised how relieved she was at seeing the familiar surroundings of *Archer Media*, and in particular *Charm*'s offices, then stopped abruptly.

She took stock of the navy velvet armchairs sat around a beautifully made oak table, white sheepskin rugs strewn across the floor, and the numerous house plants in various ceramic pots sat on a Skandi style book case, and a long sideboard which also housed a delicate set of vintage whisky decanters and tumblers.

'What is all of this?'

Charlie walked over to an enormous fern which had never been in her office before, 'and who put these things in here?' she looked around for confirmation as to why so much of her office had changed, but saw no-one. 'My office is like this, but white. Everything white. This is…this is…' she was at a loss for words and spluttered, 'horrible.' From outside of the office she heard laughter, only to find the source of it as the door opened and Mel walked in, and Charlie realised, her heart leaping, Cole next to her.

'This is too much. You know I don't need any of this,' Mel patted his arm affectionately and placed the Veuve Cliquot on the sideboard, unopened. 'Drink?' she indicated the whisky tumblers.

'It's just our way of saying thank you – that and the big bonus in your salary this month,' he laughed, 'you deserve it after what you've done for the magazine. Spend it on your children. Have an incredible Christmas.' he broke off as he watched Mel begin to pour generous drams of golden liquor, placing the stopper back carefully, 'I'm not sure I should, what with…'

'Oh come on, it's only one. And anyway, you'll probably need a drop of courage before the ceremony begins. I can't imagine how painful this past year has been for you.' Charlie watched as the tips of Cole's ears reddened in a way which she'd always found endearing. The two walked over to the armchairs and sank gratefully into them.

'I can't believe it's been a year.' Mel sipped her whisky thoughtfully, 'I know I've struggled.'

Cole shook his head. 'You've been incredible. The whole board is behind you, I know you got the job in difficult circumstances, but you've been…' Cole's voice disappeared as understanding dawned for Charlie.

'She's editor of *Charm* magazine?'

Yesssssss.

Charlie whipped her head round quickly to see who'd replied, then wished she hadn't.

'You.'

The skeletal figure had to be eight foot, or even taller. They rose so high their head hit the ceiling, causing them to stoop a little. This pushed the already foreboding, dark-as-night hooded cape over their face even further, lending them an even more menacing air.

Charlie watched as a hand that looked like a real life X-Ray protruded out of an oversized sleeve, which was - she couldn't help notice, very Autumn/Winter 2016 and really quite passé - and pointed it directly at her.

'What?'

The hooded figure said nothing. Simply waited.

'Me? What? What do you want me to do?' Charlie watched as the hand moved and pointed in the direction of her once friend and past boyfriend sitting together, toasting their success.

'What?' Mel? You want me to go to Mel?' she shook her head, exasperated, and did as she thought Death wanted. Walking past Mel's desk she spotted a photo of her friend, with James and the three children stood outside a house, surrounded by countryside with the biggest beaming smiles. Looking from the photo she noticed a window on Mel's computer which hadn't been closed. Moving closer, Charlie gasped.

For the first time in its history, *Charm* had a black and white cover. And not just that, the cover girl was *her*. Charlie fell back reeling. It was the photo she'd had taken at her desk the day before the accident. A photo which was meant to be used for a business magazine. A time before accidents. And ghost children. And Death.

She read the words on the front of the magazine -

In memoriam, an anniversary tribute to Charm *Editor Charlie Kenzie*

'No. It can't be. I told you I don't want this. This isn't happening.' As she read the words, she noticed Mel and Cole standing up, readying themselves to leave and noting for the first time they were dressed head to toe black.

'Where are you going? I'm not dead. I'm here.' She stood as close as she could next to Cole, recognising that even with the fatigue around his green eyes, he still had a look which could make her melt.

How she wished she'd been honest with him.

'Cole. I'm sorry. I'm so, so, sorry. How did I let us get to this? I'm sorry I pushed you away. I'm sorry I didn't listen. I can understand it now, you were pushing me away so I'd go to uni and not hang around, waiting for you. But I did it anyway, didn't I? Even when you got together with Kate, when you were expecting Poppy I still loved you. But by the time you'd decided to divorce Kate I'd lost sight of my love and it had twisted to hatred. Of you. Of her. Of your daughter, oh.' She clapped her hand to her mouth, 'where is Poppy? Did she survive?'

She looked for the hooded figure, who stood silently by the office door.

'Speak,' she demanded, 'tell me of Poppy – is she okay? Did she survive?'

Silence. Charlie was starting to shake with fear and worry.

In the distance she could hear bells tolling.

'I mean it. Tell me. She wasn't meant to be by that cab – she wasn't meant to be knocked down, Bow told me himself. Something happened that shouldn't have. This,' she waved at the air to try and indicate her predicament, 'was all meant for me – none of it was her fault.'

She looked closer at the magazine article for the first time and noticed a feature teaser -

My daughter, my world, by Cole Barnes.

Charlie sunk to her knees and howled.

The sound of bells was getting louder and louder, filling her ears, rolling in her heart. Filling her up, but it was too much. Too loud. She clutched her head, willing the sound to stop throbbing in her temples.

'She's not the mean, arrogant, hateful person. I am. Me. Please don't tell me she died because of me. She's the kind one. She even organised a party for sick kids, she was always so caring. Please. Don't let it be both of us – for Cole's sake.'

Chapter Twenty-One

Christmas Eve, present day

Poppy woke up.

Her body ached and she was thirstier than she'd been her whole life, including the time when Charlie had worked her so hard when they were shooting a bikini spread on a beach that she went the whole day with nothing to drink.

'There she is,' her dad's voice came from her left and Poppy smiled up at him.

'Hey,' she croaked and he immediately grabbed a bottle of water with a straw plunged into it, and put his finger to his lips.

'Shush, don't try to talk. Just have a sip of this.' Poppy did as she was told and sipped slowly, coughing as the water hit the back of her throat, but hungrily needing more. 'Done?' she nodded and rested her head back on her pillow, 'you've had a bit of a knock, but you're going to be alright. Do you know what day it is?' Her dad's face looked strained and he wore what looked to be the remnants of a Santa costume.

'Christmas Eve?' she took a guess and he smiled.

'Yes, well done. Do you remember what happened?'

She thought for a moment. Everything was fuzzy.

'I met a man called Nick, I think,' her dad's forehead furrowed, 'and I saw you – but you were younger, so sort of you but not really. But I wasn't really there,' she faltered as he looked more concerned.

He scratched his head and smiled.

'You've had a nasty bump to the head. A cab hit you earlier

this evening, you've been in and out of consciousness, but you're back now and everything is looking normal,' he smiled up at a blonde nurse, 'isn't she?'

'Yep, all good here. We won't turf you out tonight as you've had quite the knock, but you should be able to go home with your family tomorrow morning, for Christmas Day,' she smiled, tucking back a bit of tinsel that was wrapped around her head like a halo, behind her ear.

Poppy couldn't shake the thought she was missing something until suddenly she remembered.

'Was I the only person in the accident?' her dad's face crumpled as a reply and she reached a hand with an IV drip embedded into it up to him, to try and offer sympathy.

'Look, sweetie. I wasn't going to say anything until you were up to it, but it's Charlie – she was also there and, well, she's in surgery and we're being told we'll just have to wait and see. It's not looking good.' Her dad looked older than the last time she'd seen him, and then from nowhere, a realisation hit Poppy.

'You love her, don't you?'

He looked up from where his head had been in his hands.

'What? No. I'm just…' he broke off and looked out towards the window, as if the answer lay in the lights of the traffic far below.

'You do. You've always loved her. And she loves you,' Poppy realised with a surprise, unsure where her knowledge had come from, 'but you've both pushed each other way for years. Hurting each other and,' she stopped as her mum walked in, carrying on in a low voice only Cole could hear, 'and other people in the process.'

'I'm sorry,' he whispered, 'but if tonight has taught me anything it's that I need to be there for you, whatever you need. I'm not around enough and I don't say it enough, but I love you kiddo,' he kissed her on the cheek and Poppy smiled.

'You've been around for me enough. You and mum both have – I'm incredibly lucky, I have two divorced parents who still like each other. Who are still friends. But Charlie,' she broke off, remembering a room with *Take That* posters and tears outside a seaside pub, 'she doesn't have anyone and needs to hear that too. Give her something to pull through for.'

Her dad stared at her, confusion etched on his face which Poppy knew she'd never be able to explain. She couldn't fully understand it herself, but she knew Charlie needed Cole more than she did right then.

Her mum came over to them with two cups of coffee and handed one to Cole, relief on her face when she saw Poppy was awake.

'What are you two up to? Plotting?' she said, smiling and kissed Poppy's forehead, 'glad you're awake and talking darling, you gave us all a fright – what were you thinking of?'

'Tell her dad,' Poppy whispered and she was certain she saw him give a faint nod, then turned to her mum, 'sorry I ruined your party.'

Her mum smiled sadly.

'Darling, you're far more important than any party.'

'Even one when you've booked The Cocktail Guyz?' Poppy grinned at her mum's mortification.

'Even one of those. And anyway,' she looked at her ex-husband, 'I don't think now is a good time for a party.'

'Think that's your cue to go dad,' Poppy yawned, 'I won't be doing anything interesting for a while, 'cept sleeping,' she yawned again, 'when I wake up, I want to hear you did the right thing.'

Chapter Twenty-Two

Christmas Eve, present day

'She's heavily sedated,' a voice near to Charlie spoke softly, 'don't stay too long.'

'I won't,' Charlie noted Cole's voice from far away. There was a scraping of a chair whilst she floated on an island of warm bliss.

'Hey Charlotte. It's me,' he spoke quietly to her, and when he gained no response she felt a tug under the bedsheet as he found her hand and held it in his.

'Missed you,' he whispered, stroking her arm gently, 'gave us a little fright back there though,' he began.

'I'd say,' Charlie recognised her mum's voice and tried to rearrange her jumbled thoughts. Just now she'd been confronting Death – offering herself in place of Poppy. Now she seemed to be back in the hospital bed. Maybe she'd been there all this time. But what had happened to Poppy?

'We've both been through the ringer a bit this evening, haven't we? Mind you, looks like Charlie took the brunt of it,' Cole carried on speaking with her mum.

'Mmm, she's been in and out of consciousness this evening. It was the strangest thing though, when they took her into surgery – after she went from holding my hand to flat-lining – the surgeons said whilst they were all prepping one of the nurses thought they heard bells. When they'd turned back to Charlie, her monitor was showing a strong heartbeat. They did a lot of scans on her brain and nothing. No swelling. Nothing. She's basically fine,' Charlie's mum sounded relieved, 'as fine as you can be if you've been knocked down by a car.'

'Huh, odd.'

'Is your daughter okay?'

Charlie waited. This was it. This was when she found out whether she'd rescued the girl, the one she'd seen only moments before being whisked into surgery. Was it moments? Maybe the ordeal had been for hours.

She couldn't reason when her evening had started or whether it was coming to an end. All she knew was that she'd seen what could have been, what the future held and she didn't want to be that Charlie anymore. She didn't mind if Cole wanted to give her job to Mel, Mel would be better at it anyway, she realised. And more deserving. She was beginning to realise she needed to look at other options for her future.

There was only one life, she didn't want to spend the next part of it hating everything as much as she had the first part.

She needed a chance to be with her parents more and find out how good a Father Christmas her dad truly was. In a nutshell, Charlie was desperately waiting to find out if she had a second chance.

'She's much better, thank you. A few bruises – but she'll live,' Cole's voice rasped with emotion and Charlie had an overwhelming urge to wake up and kiss him.

So she did.

Chapter Twenty-Three

Christmas Day, one year later

'Room for one more?' the intercom buzzed and Charlie tried to answer it whilst holding a glass of fizz in one hand, a tray of mince pies in the other and continuing a conversation with her mum.

'Depends who's asking?' she said, smiling down the camera.

'Your fiancé, and he's freezing.' Laughing, she hit the button to let Cole in and returned to her kitchen. Smiling at the sight of her dad in his full Father Christmas costume peeling carrots with her mum, she heaved Mel's daughter Bella, up in the air.

'No more of those young lady,' she said, grinning and kissing the little girl's nose, 'mummy will not be happy if she finds out you've been scoffing all the chocolates before she gets here.' Bella looked solemnly at Charlie.

'But we won't tell her, will we Auntie C?' she cocked her head onto one side, making Charlie laugh. She doted on the girl – and the other two of course. They all knew they could get away with anything if they called her auntie. Placing the little girl on the floor and giving her a mince pie to run off with, Charlie joined her parents.

'Dad, I think maybe now's a good time for Father Christmas to hand out some presents? I think the natives are getting restless,' she grinned at the children all hovering expectantly around the tower of presents sat around and under the lush Christmas tree, she and Cole had chosen. She'd decorated it with hundreds of twinkling white lights, popcorn string – which she noted Bella was eating, and as many bells as she could find. They all lightly trilled whenever a gust of wind passed through and, rather than finding it in anyway sinister, Charlie was charmed and soothed by the sound.

'Look who I found in the entrance,' Cole said as he arrived with Poppy and Ralph, who had been inseparable the past year, swiftly followed by Melanie and James.

'Sorry we're late, have they been okay?' Mel asked, plonking the many bags down in the kitchen and James following suit.

'They've been excellent – as long as you count eating all the chocolates and chanting "we want our presents",' Charlie said, grinning at Mel's crestfallen face, 'I'm kidding, they've been great. Thanks for sorting the turkey, not a clue why I couldn't get it to cook here.'

It was Mel's turn to smile.

'Is it because until a year ago you'd never used this kitchen to cook in, and for the past 12 months you've had so many parties and lunches and whatnot, the poor oven doesn't know what's hit it?'

'Maybe.' Charlie grabbed a glass and filled it with some champagne for her friend.

'I forgot to say, Cole showed me the January proofs,' she took a sip of her drink and, despite enjoying the bubbles as they popped on her tongue, kept her face stern.

Mel looked concerned, waiting to hear her thoughts.

'And?'

Charlie grinned

'And I thought it was brilliant. Beautiful. Bold. I'm completely flattered you put me on the front – black and white did me many favours,' she laughed, and Mel's face lit up.

'Charlie you deserve to be our *Woman of the Year*. Look at how much you've achieved,' Mel clinked her glass with her, 'setting up *Secret Santa* has been the most incredible mission.'

Shaking her head, Charlie nodded in the direction of her mum.

'I only took what she was doing on a local offering and scaled it up a bit.'

'Oh no, you're not getting away with that. You turned it national. To match up people who were in need of some love and a gift, with someone who could provide it, whether they're young or old. It's brilliant and your powers of persuasion brought on all those toy manufacturers and supermarkets. You're changing people's lives. Making things better.'

She pulled Charlie in for a hug, something the two hadn't stopped doing for the last few months.

'I've said it before, but that knock on the head did you a world of good.'

Sipping her drink, and watching her friends and family in her home, Charlie smiled.

'More than you'll ever know.'

The End

Afterword

It's a sad fact, but many children have to experience Christmasses in place unfit for them (and their parents).
Whilst Charlie's charity *Secret Santa* doesn't exist, there are many out there who work tirelessly to provide some festive cheer for people at Christmas.

If you want to help, here are some of the charities in the UK who would happily accept your donation.
Alternatively, why not look for groups in your local area and see if someone closer to home is need of your help this season.

Merry Christmas, and thank you.

Holly
xxx

The Salvation Army
https://www.salvationarmy.org.uk/christmas-present-appeal

The Book Trust
https://www.booktrust.org.uk/support-us/give-ten-pounds-today-and-bring-joy-to-a-vulnerable-child-this-christmas/

Crisis
https://www.crisis.org.uk/crisis-at-christmas/

The Trussell Trust
https://www.trusselltrust.org/get-involved/ways-to-give/

Age UK
https://www.ageuk.org.uk/get-involved/donate/

Acknowledgements

First, thanks must go to you, the reader. I know you have a lot of choice out there, so thank you for deciding on Secret Santa, if you liked it, please leave a review on Amazon. This is the first in a series of Secret books, so keep your eyes peeled for the next one, Secret Valentine, out late January 2024.

Thanks to my publisher, Blue Pier Books, for putting so much love and thought into my books.

Thanks to my friends, Charley and Michelle for putting up with numerous Christmas related questions when it was boiling hot.

Thank you to my husband and son for giving their feedback on all things 'lovey dovey', and coping with the numerous iterations I'd discuss over the dinner table.

And finally, thanks to my incredible daughter, Miss B, who has become my official proofreader, first reader and general supporter of all things *Secret*. I think we deserve a hot chocolate with gingerbread men. Don't you? x

Recipes

Lots of the characters in *Secret Santa* enjoy a Christmas drink and snack. Below are three of their favourites.

Poppy's Hot Chocolate

Makes four glasses, takes 15 minutes

Ingredients

700ml semi-skimmed milk
1 tbsp vanilla extract
200g white chocolate, chopped into small pieces
Pink gel food colouring
Marshmallows, whipped cream and mini gingerbread men

Method

Place the milk, vanilla and chopped white chocolate in a medium saucepan and simmer on a medium heat, stirring occasionally with a whisk, until the white chocolate has melted.
Add one drop of pink food colouring just before the mixtures comes to the boil, remove the pan from the heat and serve immediately.

Top with whipped cream, marshmallows and gingerbread men – enjoy!

Maggie's Mulled Wine

Serves 6-8, takes about 20 minutes

Ingredients

1 lemon
2 oranges
8 cloves
2 cinnamon sticks
4cm (1.5in) piece ginger, peeled and sliced
60g (2½oz) light brown sugar
60ml ruby port
75cl bottle full-bodied red wine
For the garnish
½ orange, sliced into half moons
½ lemon, sliced into half moons
6-8 cinnamon sticks

Method

Using a potato peeler, remove the zest from the lemon and one of the oranges in thin strips then juice the zested orange. Push the cloves into the remaining orange.
Put the zest, orange juice and clove studded orange in a large pan along with 2 cinnamon sticks, the ginger, sugar, port, red wine and 750ml (1 1/2 pint) water.

Put over a low heat and stir until the sugar dissolves, then turn up the heat slightly and simmer gently for 20 minutes.

Remove from the heat and leave to cool for 10 minutes before ladling into glasses.

Garnish with the orange and lemon slices and a cinnamon stick.

Ladle into chipped mugs or fancy ones!

Nick's Mince Pies

Ingredients
For the pastry
175g/6oz plain flour
75g/2½oz cold butter, cubed
25g/1oz icing sugar, plus extra for dusting
1 large orange, grated zest only
1 free-range egg, beaten

For the filling
250g/9oz good-quality ready-made mincemeat
100g/3½oz ready-to-eat dried apricots, finely chopped (do this in a food processor if you're short on time)
125g/4oz uncoloured marzipan, grated

Method
Preheat the oven to 200C/180C Fan/Gas 6 and place a baking sheet inside to heat up.

For the pastry, either pulse the flour and butter in a food processor until the mixture resembles breadcrumbs, or rub the flour and butter together in a large bowl using your fingertips.

Stir in the icing sugar and orange zest, then stir in the beaten egg and mix until the ingredients just come together as a dough. Wrap the dough in greaseproof paper and chill in the fridge for 10-15 minutes, or until firm.

When the pastry has rested, unwrap it. Place the greaseproof paper on a work surface and lightly dust with icing sugar. Place the dough on top, dust with icing sugar, then cover with another sheet of greaseproof paper. Roll the pastry between the sheets of greaseproof paper to a thickness of 1-2mm.

Stamp 12 rounds from the pastry using a 8cm/3in fluted pastry cutter.

Line each hole of the muffin tin with one of the pastry rounds and prick the base of each with a fork.

For the filling, mix the mincemeat with the chopped apricots until well combined. Divide the mixture equally among the pastry cases. Top each tart with some of the grated marzipan.

Slide the muffin tin onto the hot baking sheet and bake in the oven for 12-15 minutes, or until golden-brown and crisp.

Dust with icing sugar and serve warm (good to line your pockets if you're in *A Christmas Carol*)

About The Author

Holly Green

Holly is a an avid watcher of all Christmas Hallmark movies, and is a sucker for rom coms where everything is happy ever after.

She lives in West Sussex with her two children, ever suffering husband and always sleeping dog. She's excited to create the Secret series, and hopes readers will enjoy discovering all that is Secret!

Printed in Great Britain
by Amazon

30563221R00078